Totally Bound Publishing books by Amelia Kingston

So Far, So Good
So, That Got Weird
This is So Happening

I0542075

So Far, So Good

THIS IS SO HAPPENING

AMELIA KINGSTON

THIS IS SO
HAPPENING

Dedication

To Layla.
The light of my life. The center of my universe.
The reason I get out of bed in the morning.
You're not a dog, you're a furry therapist.
Thank you for the cuddles and kisses.
You can't read this, but walkies and extra treats
are coming your way.

Chapter One

Jessie

I tap my sneaker on the faded tile floor of the auditorium and check the clock for the tenth time in thirty seconds. Perched on the last two inches of my seat, my butt nearly sliding off the curved plastic edge, I sling my backpack over my shoulder and eye the exit fifteen feet away. *If I'm quick, he won't even notice me leave.*

Don't judge.

I love my Marketing Principles class, but Professor Pfeffer always ends ten minutes early. *Always.* That's why he's my favorite. Well, that, and because his name is so fun to say.

He's got to be about done, right? Professor P. reaches into his briefcase and pulls out a notepad. *I guess not.* He's rambling about some end-of-term project and, while I'm sure it's important, I've got to go. Today — like every day — I've got more to do than I've got hours to do it.

When Professor P. turns to the whiteboard, I make a break for it. I'm up the aisle and out of the door in a flash. *I'll just grab the notes from Austin later.*

I close my eyes and turn my face up to the warm sun, taking a deep breath and reveling in the chilly air filling my lungs after two hours in that stuffy lecture. I bask in the sunshine for a full two seconds, then tighten my high ponytail and get moving. I grab a protein bar, my cell and my headphones out of my bag before throwing it over my shoulder.

The three missed texts from Maddy are no surprise, but guilt still churns in my empty stomach. I take a big bite of my protein bar and head off towards the baseball field at an easy run. I'm going to have to book it if I don't want to be late to intramural kickball.

I shoot a quick text letting Maddy know I'm on my way, before tapping my mom's smiling face in my contacts. I slip my headphones in and listen to the ringing.

"Birdie!" My mom greets me with my childhood nickname.

"Hey, Mom. Sorry I missed your call yesterday. School's been pretty crazy. Getting ready for finals and everything." I breathe out through my nose to avoid panting into the microphone.

"Oh, don't worry about me. I know how busy you kids get."

Liar, liar, pants on fire. Missing the weekly call from Mom is dangerous territory. It isn't done in the Allen clan. We're a pretty tightknit group thanks to Mom's kung-fu grip on those family ties.

"How's school?" Mom asks.

"Great. Busy, but great. I'm heading over to a kickball game right now."

"What fun," Mom chirps. A quick beat passes, her maternal senses obviously tingling. "Jessie, honey, are you okay? You're breathing a little hard."

"Just a little pre-game warm-up jog." I grab my headphones and hold the mic away from my mouth.

"You're not trying to do too much at once, are you?"

I swallow the last bite of my protein bar dinner and deflect. "Me? Never." I glance at the time on my phone and pick up my pace.

"Jessica Bridget Allen…"

I cringe at my full name.

"You know me, I'm a multitasker," I quip. She sighs. *Time to go on the offensive.* "How's everything with you? You and Dad decide what color to paint the kitchen?"

It's an underhanded trick to bring up the never-ending remodel, a topic of heated debates between my parents for the past six months. Without fail, my mom launches into her latest argument in favor of chartreuse, a color my dad is convinced belongs nowhere but in a margarita glass. He's right of course, but all of us Allen children are smart enough not to pick sides in this one.

The baseball field comes into view and I slow down to a brisk walk.

"I absolutely get it. Who wouldn't want their kitchen painted to symbolize happiness and nature?" I placate Mom as I wave to Maddy to prove I made it. "Look, Mom, I better get going. The game is about to start."

"Right, right. Good luck. Oh, and don't forget brunch this weekend. Jake is bringing a new girl for us to meet."

"A new one? What happened to the one from last month? What was her name, Rachel?"

My mom lets out a deep breath. "I can't keep track of them, to be honest."

We share a laugh at my precocious middle brother's expense.

"When are you going to bring someone home to us, Jessie Bird?"

Not any time soon. Who has time for a serious boyfriend in college? Between sorority duties, intramural sports, study groups, homework and oh yeah, going to class, I sure as hell don't.

"My team captain is waving at me frantically. I gotta get going. Love you, Mom."

"Love you too, sweetie."

I shove my headphones into my backpack, grab my team T-shirt and pull it on over my tank top. It's fifty degrees outside, but I don't regret forgoing a sweatshirt. I've always been hot-blooded. Dad swears it's because I never sit still.

"Thank god you're finally here," Maddy's exasperated voice calls out across the field. "You're late."

I greet the grumpy co-ed with a bright smile. "Nice to see you too, Maddy. Class ran longer than expected." I check the time. Five twenty-three. Less than half an hour late is early for me.

Maddy gives me a soft smile. "Sorry, it's just half the guys who said they'd come haven't shown up and we were going to have to forfeit if you didn't make it."

I look over at our withering bench, full of bored and anxious faces. I take a breath and step up the pep. *Time to get this derailed party train back on track.* I grab Maddy's shoulders and give her a shake. "It's college kickball. Not the Olympics. Lighten up." I add a little hip check. "Shall we get this show on the road?"

I strut to the dugout, toss a fist into the air and cheer. "Who's ready to get their kickball on?" I'm greeted with muted enthusiasm. I do some exaggerated kicking motion stretches with my long legs while making old-man-grunting noises. "You all need to bring your A-game. Can't have you embarrassing me in front of the scouts."

"Scouts?" Terrance snickers.

I brush the imaginary chip off my shoulder. "Yeah. I'm lookin' to go pro. You didn't know? I'm *huge* in Japan," I deadpan. That does it. The whole team cracks up and we're chugging along to Fun Town.

Seven innings, a victory and a quick shower later, I'm texting Trevor that I'm on my way and speed-walking to the library. A few people from my Econ class are hunkered down at a table in the very back for our regular study group.

I stroll up, throw my arms out wide and declare, "I have arrived. Let the learning begin." I get a couple of chuckles and a few sighs. *Worth it.*

We're packing it in an hour later and my phone buzzes with a call from Hannah, my sorority's president.

"What's up, Hannah Banana?"

"Hey, Jessie! So, you know we've got that charity event this weekend?"

I wave to Trevor and make my way to the library exit. "Yeah, at the Children's Hospital. I'll be there."

"That's great. I was talking to Sam and we were thinking it'd be great to bring cookies with us."

"Cookies?" I step out into the cold night and stroll back to my house. It's late now and the campus is quiet, only a few students scurrying to their dorms.

"Yeah, something home cooked. Hospital food is awful, and who doesn't like cookies?"

I chuckle, knowing where this is going. "I'm sure the kids would love that."

"Awesome. So, you think you could make your famous chocolate chunk cookies? I think a few dozen would be enough."

I scrunch up my face, squeezing my eyes shut tight and dropping my head back. My mind swims with all the things on my schedule right now. *It's for sick kids. How can I say no to sick kids?* I choke down an exhausted sigh.

"Sure, Hannah," I answer. "I can manage that."

"You're the best, Jessie!" she coos before hanging up.

I make it home, flop down on my bed and crack open my books. A few more hours knocking out homework and I'm finally done for the night. I slip on my favorite flannel pajama shorts, despite them being too short on me, and an oversized ratty T-shirt. Dead on my feet, I manage to drag myself to the bathroom to brush my teeth.

I realize I didn't close the door after Michelle pops her head in. Even in the sanctity of our sorority house at almost midnight, she looks put together, as always. Her cute matching pajama set hugs her petite body, her long black hair is glistening and a light coating of mascara makes those upturned brown eyes pop. She tries harder than she needs to. She's got an exotic beauty tempered by a natural sweetness that makes boys take notice. I watch her hovering behind me in the mirror, the unassuming smile on her delicate face a dead giveaway I'm about to do her a favor.

"What are you doing this weekend?" she asks innocently enough.

I narrow my eyes at her. "I've got a study group on Saturday. Then I've got a family brunch Sunday. And we've got that volunteer event for the Children's Hospital on Sunday afternoon that I'm now making a few dozen cookies for. And sometime between all that

I've got two term papers to write," I ramble off my schedule, already tired. Michelle nods behind me, biting her lip. I make the mistake of asking, "Why?"

"Nothing. You're busy…" She leans against the sink next to me and sighs.

"Never too busy for one of my sisters," I tell her earnestly.

She pounces. "Will you come to the party with me on Saturday?"

Okay, I'll admit, I walked right into this one.

"The one at the football house?" I ask.

She nods, dropping her chin to her chest and staring at me with those big puppy-dog eyes.

"I thought you and Monte were over?"

"We are. Beyond over. The guy's a jerk."

I shake my head and stumble back to my room, Michelle hot on my heels. "Then why would you want to go to a party at *his* house?"

"To show him that I'm over him. Duh," she answers with a sassy head wobble. She plops down on my bed, flipping through my statistics textbook. "Besides, the season is almost over. It's going to be one of the best parties of the year."

I take the textbook from her and stack it with its many friends on my desk. "I don't know," I answer, pulling back the covers and telegraphing my deep desire to go to sleep. Michelle doesn't take the hint.

"I need a wing woman." She slouches, her slender shoulders folding forward. She pretends nothing rattles her, but she is more insecure than people would ever guess. "Please?" she asks, her voice soft.

We both know I'm going to say yes. All I'm doing is losing precious sleep pretending otherwise.

"Okay. Okay. I'll come."

"Thank you! You're the best." She hops off the bed and throws her arms around me, squeezing tight.

"So I've heard. Now go away, I need my beauty sleep!"

She skips away, singing her thank-yous as she does.

I close the door behind her and sigh. It's past midnight when I collapse in bed, after setting my alarm for six a.m. to get up and do it all over again.

Chapter Two

Devin

The alarm on my phone blares in my ear and I silence it with a grunt, dragging my tired ass out of bed before the damn sun is up. After shaking some of the stiffness from my muscles, and pulling on a pair of worn but clean jeans, I lurch into the kitchen for some much-needed coffee.

I'm too young to be this sore in the mornings. I swear, sometimes I feel a hundred years old. *Never had this problem when I spent my days under the hood of a car.* It's sitting in that damn office, hunched over a mountain of invoices and staring at a dim computer screen until I can't see straight. Humans weren't meant to do this shit. A man should have something to show for himself at the end of the day. Something tangible.

Pouring myself a strong cup of fresh-brewed dark roast, I run through the day ahead of me. It's Saturday, so the shop is going to be a madhouse. Sean's got to repair the engine on that Jeep. I need that bay for the

Chevy I've got coming in for a service. I've got to call Jose over at the junk yard to see if he's got anything we can use to fix that piece-of-crap Pontiac Mrs. Jensen keeps bringing in. How the old woman can even still see over the steering wheel is beyond me. I'll have to place a new order with Mikulski's today for some brake pads and rotors before we get too low. Then there's next week's schedule to write. *Does Shelley want Tuesday or Wednesday off?*

I take another sip of coffee, the warm bitter taste doing its part in cutting through the morning haze. I fucking hate mornings.

I get to the shop before anyone else, like usual, and start flipping on the lights. The smell of grease and gas welcomes me, sweeter than the finest perfume. We don't open for another two hours, but I can get a lot more work done when I don't have to man the counter as well. The old metal office chair groans underneath me when I lower my massive frame into it. *I know the feeling.* I don't want to be sitting here all day either. We've all got shit we'd rather not do. That's called life. *Better get used to it.*

The quiet of the small office — and my productivity — is shattered by the sound of mechanics busting through the door.

"I've been fixin' cars since you were just a wriggling sperm in your daddy's ball sac, you little punk," Shelley calls out across the shop. She's been giving our new guy, Mikey, shit since he started a year ago. He's a few years younger than me, in his early twenties, but he's baby-faced and naive as fuck. *An easy target.*

"And you look it too," Mikey taunts back. *Dumb move, kid.* I'm pretty sure Shelley's killed a few men before. I bet they were all assholes that deserved it, but point is not to fuck with a woman who knows where to hide bodies.

"The fuck you just say to me? You're asking to get your ass beat, boy!"

Childish giggling is followed by the unmistakable clatter of tools hitting a cement floor.

Sean, the older and calmer one, chimes in with, "Don't kill 'em, Shel. He's so pretty to look at."

I grumble at their bullshit, despite indulging in a small smile that no one can see while I'm hunkered down in the office. "Knock that shit off before customers show up!" I shout at them like a dad threatening to turn the car around.

The scuffling continues, although a bit muted now. At least they're trying to hide it, which is something. A knock on the door draws my attention to Sean waiting to talk to me.

"Got a second, boss?" he asks.

I'm not the boss, but I run the place, so that's what everyone calls me.

"Sure. What's up?" I ask the weathered old mechanic.

"I was hoping to take Tuesday off next week."

I push down a sigh. So much for that fucking schedule I spent an hour making this morning.

"I would, but Shelley asked for Tuesday off first."

Sean's head tilts to the side and he calls out, "Shel, you want Tuesday or Wednesday off?"

"Wednesday. Championship for league bowling night," Shelley calls back.

"Well, fuck. I guess that's sorted then." I tear up the schedule and start writing a new one from scratch.

"You all right, boss? You look like shit." Sean means well, but I don't have time for this. Doesn't matter if I'm all right or not — shit still needs to get done and there's no one else to do it.

"Yeah, Sean. I'm fine. You can have Tuesday off, but I'll need you to work overtime on Wednesday so Shelley can go to her league night."

"No problem. Thanks, Dev."

Sean disappears and I focus again on the million other things I've got to get done today. I growl at the unwelcome sound of my phone buzzing. *What the fuck is it now?*

"What?" I answer.

"Good morning to you too, sunshine!" Austin, my best friend and colossal pain in my ass, sings out. "You need to get laid, man. Bad."

"I got work to do. This call have a point?"

Austin laughs. "You coming to my game tonight?"

Damn. I look over at my calendar and remember his family night game is tonight. Austin and I give each other no end of shit, but I love the guy like a brother. I'm the only family he has and I sure as fuck need to make it to his game tonight.

"What time?"

"Game starts at six. After party starts at ten."

If I have one of the guys close up for me, I'll make it. I'll be late, but I have to be there.

"I'll make the second half. But I'm not going to a fucking college party," I tell him.

"Fine. Let your dick shrivel up and fall off." I'd bet money Austin has that smug smirk on his face that makes me wonder what it'd feel like to smack him. "Elizabeth will be in my section, so be nice. Well, as nice as you ever are anyway."

Elizabeth is Austin's quasi-girlfriend sort-of boss. He told about her and their weird 'sex tutor' arrangement. He keeps saying it's just a job, but he's at least half in love with her already. It's going to end badly. Love always does.

* * * *

I pull my eyes away from the two chicks grinding against each other in Austin's living room to grab the beer he holds out. I take a long sip and try to relax. This isn't my scene. College was never an option for me. Hell, I barely graduated high school. I'm a couple of years older than these kids, but I've seen a lot more of the real world than any of them ever will. Except maybe Austin. My best friend's had his fair share of sucker punches in life. Still, he always fits in. He's made a fucking art form out of it. Me? I couldn't care less.

His eyes are locked on the front door, like he can will Elizabeth to appear in front of him. I've never seen him like this. He's fucking gone for this girl.

"What's up with you two?" I ask, knowing he won't give me a straight answer.

"Nothing. She's just a friend." He shakes his head with a rueful smile and takes a swig of beer.

"You sticking your tongue down your friends' throats now? Fair warning, I had onions for dinner," I deadpan.

He picks at the label to his beer bottle and mutters, "Fuck off. It's complicated."

"No shit. You need to be careful with that girl." I don't think he realizes he's in love yet.

"Still afraid I'm going to break her? Don't worry, she's tougher than she looks."

I nod. "No doubt. I'm more worried about her breaking you, bro." I think back to Austin's football game earlier tonight, when he looked up to see Elizabeth in the stands, decked out in school colors, wearing his jersey and cheering him on. He's never had that. *Support. Family. Love.* I'm not sure what he'll do if he loses it. "I saw the look on your face when you saw her in the stands tonight."

He doesn't answer. Instead, he waves over a distraction. She's blonde and beautiful. *Striking.* A wide and friendly smile lights up her face and she winks. My chest tightens. She takes her time walking over to us, letting me appreciate the curvy body that goes along with that beautiful face. She's on the conservative side for this party, jeans and a T-shirt, but with a body like hers she doesn't need to show skin to be sexy as hell. I resist the urge to shift in my seat.

"Hey, Austin. Who's your friend?" she asks him, but her eyes are locked on mine. They're a cool, deep green with a mischievous glint that matches the playful lift of her rosy lips. I take a long drag of my beer, not bothering to answer.

"This is Devin. Rhymes with heaven, but he's closer to the devil," Austin quips. I hate his smart ass. I level him with a glare and the fucker just laughs.

The girl's soft voice drags my attention back to her. "I'm Jessica. Jessie." She smiles at me and small dimples appear on each cheek. I swallow hard. "Are you a transfer? I don't think I've seen you on campus before."

"Not a student." I stare through her.

She keeps right on smiling. "Just visiting? It's an awesome campus. I can show you around sometime if you want. How long are you going to be here for?"

I ignore her, waiting for her to get bored.

"Devin's a local boy. But I'm sure he'd love to be shown around some of your sights," Austin pipes in.

I debate punching my best friend in the face when a loud crash draws our attention to the other side of the room, where some guy just took a swan dive off the pool table. In the packed space, it causes a chain reaction of people falling like dominoes. Limbs are flailing, followed by the sounds of bodies hitting the floor with grunts and groans. Jessie's smile drops as she takes in the chaos. Just before the human wreckage reaches us, I wrap an arm around her and pull her against me. Her hands land on my chest and she lets out a quick gasp at my manhandling. The guy next to her tumbles over, spilling a drink on the carpet where she was just standing.

I sweep my eyes over Jessie, looking for any damage. She looks unscathed. Those dimples are back in her pink cheeks. "Thanks," she purrs, tucking a strand of blonde hair behind her ear. My pulse kicks up.

I purse my lips and give a quick nod. I should let her go, but I don't. She doesn't pull away either.

Chapter Three

Jessie

Devin's heartbeat is fast but steady under my palm. My own heart is racing at the sensation of being held against his hard body. He looks disinterested and annoyed, surveying the crowd around us. Even with that scowl affixed to his face, he's devastatingly handsome. Despite sitting next to Austin Jacobs, considered one of the hottest guys on campus, Devin stands out. I couldn't take my eyes off him from across the room. He's tall and broad. Muscular in an everyday sort of way, not in the I-work-out-can-you-tell kind of way. His deep olive skin, black hair and dark eyes give him a mysterious appearance. Wearing weathered work boots, dark jeans and a long-sleeved black Henley pushed up to his elbows, he looks like he'd be more comfortable on a construction site than at this party.

His jaw is clenched tight and he's wearing a deep frown. He looks detached, almost angry, the practiced emotion etched into every inch of his hard features. But his eyes tell a different story. There's a gentleness and hesitation in them. I resist the urge to run my fingers along the scruff at his square jaw or over the dark tattoos that line his arms. I have a sudden and unexplainable need to hear him laugh. I bet he's unfathomably beautiful when he's happy.

"Looks like I have my very own knight in shining armor," I coo. "Thanks for the assist, big man." He scoffs. *Tough crowd.*

Devin nods behind me and Austin shoots up like a rocket, his eyes locked on Elizabeth. I spin out of Devin's arms and take Austin's vacated seat. My leg is pressed against Devin's as both our gazes follow the path Austin blazes to his target. I lean into Devin, using the loud room as justification for the intimacy. Really, I just want to know if he'll pull away when I press my body against his. He doesn't. He smells amazing. Something mechanical and hard that I can't place.

"Someone's smitten," I murmur into Devin's ear.

"Him or her?"

I let out a mock gasp. "He speaks. Be still my heart."

He turns towards me slowly. I refuse to pull back, my grin locked in place. His face is less than an inch away. The bustle of the room around us fades as his dark eyes burn into mine. I pull in a long, slow breath, trying not to suffocate in the desire to kiss him. I've never felt an instant attraction like this. His gaze drops to my lips and heat pools in my stomach. I lean into him farther, my eyes fluttering closed and my nose nearly grazing his.

I can tell he snaps his head away by the swift wash of air over my heated cheeks. My eyes pop open and my jaw drops. Staring straight forward, he clears his throat and takes a slow sip of his beer.

What a damn tease.

I shake it off with a chuckle. "Both," I answer his earlier question. He nods. I have no idea if that is an agreement or just acknowledgment. "Guess it's true what they say…"

He turns to me, an eyebrow raised in question. The right side of my mouth quirks up at the sight. He's curious, even if he refuses to ask. I lean across his body and take the beer out of his hand. I keep my eyes locked on his as I take a long pull and hand it back.

"Opposites attract."

He turns his face down and stares at his beer. I can't quite tell, but I'd swear he's wearing the hint of a smile.

Something slams into my side.

"Jessie Bird!" A drunk Michelle cries into my ear. She plasters herself to me and wraps her arms around my neck. "I've been looking for you all night."

She hasn't been. After begging me to be her wing woman, she ditched me to spend the night with Andrew Wright, most of it with her tongue down his throat. Drew is the team's star defensive back, a corn-fed country boy about the size of a Mack truck. He's entering the NFL draft in a few months and I have no doubt he'll have a Super Bowl ring some day.

"Oh yeah? What's up, babe?" I ask, gripping her waist to keep her steady. She sways into me and I fall against Devin. He wraps his arm around my back, resting on my far hip. Unfortunately, it feels more reassuring than intimate.

"We won." Michelle throws her arms up in excitement.

"I know. I saw."

"I told Drew he had a good game." Her voice is soft and wistful. "He's so nice. Don't you think he's nice?"

"Yes, he's nice. I saw you congratulating him," I tease.

"We were talking." *They were making out.* "But Kimmie made me go do shots and now I can't find him." She pouts.

Unsteady, she stumbles and starts to take me with her. Devin's hold tightens on my hip, grounding me. He's strong and stable at my back. My heart flutters at the sensation. Michelle shifts her eyes between me and Devin before narrowing on me. She pokes me in the chest, right above my racing heart. "Lisssteeen to meee, Jethie Birwd—" She draws out her words and slurs my nickname. "You know what you want, so you better go and you get it! You. *Get.* It." A hard jab from those manicured nails punctuates every word. "Screw what everyone else thinks. Bunch'a punks anyway."

"Okay, Dalai Lama. How 'bout we get you some water and a ride home?"

I stand up and slide my arm around Michelle. Missing the feel of Devin close behind me, I turn and give him a quick, apologetic smile. He lifts his beer in a salute before turning his attention to the party around us.

I find Marcell, the designated driver for the night, and drop Michelle off with him as I go in search of a bottle of water for her. We manage to wrangle her into the back of Marcell's car with two other sorority sisters who've had enough for the night. I hand them each a bottle of water and promise to check in on them later.

After the car is out of sight, I turn to the party again. I'm ready to search out Devin and get that smile I'm dead set on weaseling out of him, but there's no need. He's standing on the porch watching me. The party is still raging behind him, music pouring out through the open front door. Devin is backlit by the chaos. His tall frame shrouded in darkness makes him look almost menacing. But I don't feel threatened. I'm excited. My heart skitters and I grin at him.

He shakes his head and twirls the keys in his hand. "Want a ride?"

I fan my face. "I'm swooning. That was almost a full sentence."

He stalks up to me, closing the space between us in a few broad steps. I straighten and stare up at him, undaunted. The beating of my heart drowns out the muffled ruckus of the party. My skin prickles with the crisp breeze swirling around us. My eyes soak in the shadowed lines of his face as his warm breath brushes against my cheek. He groans and walks away. I stare daggers at him strutting down the street. He gets off on rejecting me.

He slows next to an old muscle car, the kind of thing my brothers would lose their minds over. Opening the driver's-side door, he shouts at me over his shoulder, "Coming, JB?"

JB? Not Jessica. Not Jessie. Not even Jessie Bird! I get initials like some locker-room buddy. *Who is this guy?* After four years of horny jocks and handsy frat boys, detached Devin is an irresistible temptation. Being told I can't have something makes me *need* it. I love a challenge and Devin's aloofness is the ultimate aphrodisiac.

He stands there, elbows perched on the roof of the car. He's looking off down the street, but he's waiting for me. When his gaze drifts to me, I pull my hair off my shoulder with a sexy toss. I lick my lips, hoping they glisten in the moonlight, and unleash a naughty smile that hints at all the dirty thoughts running through my mind.

Without a word, I strut up to the passenger's-side door with a swing of my hips and climb in. A thud that sounds very much like a fist pounding on the roof of a muscle car makes me chuckle. Devin climbs in beside me, enveloping me in his dark demeanor and masculine smell. I inhale the citrus and gasoline scent, an intoxicating combination that makes my mouth water.

I turn to him with a simper. "If you insist."

The growl escaping his chest matches the rumble of the engine as he starts the car and pulls out into the street.

"So, Devin. Are you a car guy?"

"Which way?" he asks, avoiding my question.

I point to the right. "I'm a bit of a car person myself."

I catch Devin side-eyeing me as he turns right.

"My 2010 Civic is a classic," I tease, stealing my features. "Experts all agree Honda outdid themselves with that four-cylinder masterpiece."

He shakes his head and in the passing streetlights I can tell he's amused. Excitement courses through me with the growing desperation to make this man laugh.

"It's in near-mint condition. Aside from an unfortunate incident with a runaway shopping cart, it's cherry," I deadpan.

We come to the next stop. He nods forward. I point to the right again.

"Another few years and it will be worth a whopping three thousand dollars. Give me a call sometime if you want to take her for a spin."

He looks around as realization sets in. "Why did we circle the block?"

"That's me." I point at the house on the end of the street. "You asked if I wanted a ride, not if I had somewhere to go. Life's about the journey, not the destination."

I turn my face towards him, tilt my chin down to meet my shoulder and bat my eyelashes. I know for a fact I look adorable. He glares at me, dumbfounded. I crank it up with an eyebrow wiggle and a wink. He looks away with a soft groan that says he's more annoyed than entertained. This guy's a master at non-verbal communication. He's got more groans than Eskimos have ways to say snow.

He pulls over in front of my house, turns off the engine, saunters to my side of the car and yanks open my door.

"Such a gentleman, Big Man," I tease, patting his chest as I slip out of the car. I let my hand linger on his firm pec while I stare up into those dark eyes of his. The cool night air turns molten between us. I'm desperate for him to kiss me and I have no doubt he knows it. My heart is racing, but his face is stone. I slide my hand down his stomach, delighting in the feel of his abs tightening at my touch, before letting it drop between us. We're rooted in this standoff, a silent war raging between two near strangers. I break first. Letting out a puff of air, I shake my head and turn to walk up the path.

A deep grunt is my only warning before Devin's firm grip spins me to face him, my chest crashing against his. He slips his arm around my waist, holding me there while his other hand slides to the nape of my neck in a gentle but possessive grasp. I pull in a ragged breath. Struggling for control, I grab the hard biceps of his arm around my back and hook my other hand on his wrist near my chin. If he lets go, I might crumble.

"You talk too much." Dark eyes lure me in and warm breath tickles my lips. Devin's mouth is soft but demanding when it meets mine. He tightens his grip on me. I moan when he plunges his tongue into my mouth.

His kiss consumes me. Every cell in my body explodes with sensation. The heat of his body pressing against mine scorches my insides. He devours every inch of my restraint and I melt into him. The world fades away and all I crave is more. I'm frantic. Desperate for more of this kiss. More of his touch. More of him.

He breaks the kiss as fast as he started it. I'm still in a haze when he drives off without so much as a goodbye.

Chapter Four

Jessie

"Better put that phone away before Mom sees you." I skate past my brother Jake with a nudge. "No phones during family time."

"Better mind your own business before you fall flat on your face," he snaps in return, but he's searching the ice rink for Mom. He spots her glaring and tucks his phone away. He catches up to me and we jostle back and forth, testing each other's balance in that loving way only siblings do. My skate catches and I screech, almost falling. Jake laughs beside me. *Ah, the joy of having brothers.*

We straighten up and behave when we make it to the bench where Mom's sipping hot cocoa, waving as we pass by. Her eyes narrow in suspicion. We giggle like we're still adolescent idiots and skate away. Luckily, she's too busy with her chubby and adorable newborn grandson to chase after us.

Ice skating is a Christmas tradition for the Allen family. One of many. A mandatory event for all Allen children and any significant others.

"Where's...*Nancy*?" I ask, trying to remember his latest girlfriend's name.

"Natalie," he corrects with a sigh. "She wasn't comfortable with the meet-the-family moment. Said she isn't looking for anything serious right now."

I wince. "Ouch. Sorry, big brother." I give him a pat on the shoulder. "How about some cider? My treat."

"Special cider?"

I turn my back to our mom and pull out my flask. "Of course."

Special cider is one of the newer Allen children traditions.

"Sold."

We grab a bench and watch the skaters float by, sipping our warm apple and cinnamon deliciousness with an extra kick courtesy of my Schnapps.

"How's your last year going? Ready to be an adult?"

"Bite me," I scoff. "I'm more of an adult than you'll ever be."

"Keep dreaming, Jessie Bird."

I shake my head. "School's been a little crazy. I really needed this Christmas break."

"Pfft. You're not getting any sympathy from me. Don't even try."

"That's why you're my favorite brother. You really care," I tease with my mock little-girl voice.

"Whatever. You know you do it to yourself. Two letters. N.O. That's all it takes, Jessie."

"I say no to tons of stuff."

He narrows his eyes at me and shakes his head.

"Okay. Not *tons*." He stares at me. I shove him with my shoulder. "We can't all be cold-hearted jerks."

Jake lets out a hearty chuckle. He's an attorney for Legal Aid. *Some cold-hearted jerk.*

He hums and takes a sip of his cider. "I won't apologize for going after what I want. You're just jealous."

I let out a sharp laugh. "Jealous? You're an idiot."

"You are. You're jealous I know what I want in life and you're too busy doing shit for other people to figure yourself out."

"Calm down. You're an underpaid lawyer with an overused Tinder finger, not the second coming!"

Jake and I share another laugh and I realize how much I've missed my favorite brother. I make a mental note to carve out time to talk to him more. Somehow.

"Seriously, when was the last time you did something just because you wanted to and not because someone asked you to?"

I wave him off. "I don't know what you're talking about."

"Then you're more delusional than Jamie thinking he'll turn the music world on its head with his banjo skills."

Jake's pocket vibrates and he pulls out that stupid phone again. The words *New Match* pop up before he starts scrolling through pictures of singles near us.

"Jesus, give it a rest."

"Give what a rest?" he asks, oblivious.

I snatch his phone and shove it into my pocket.

"Hey!"

"We're all pretty sick of this revolving door of soulmates you keep dragging to family dinners." I love my brother, but he is a serial monogamist, desperate to find love. His current strategy seems to be process of elimination, working his way through the fairer sex one by one.

"Just because you hate love — "

"I do *not* hate love!"

"Bullshit," he fake-coughs.

"I don't."

"Says the girl who's never had a serious boyfriend."

"That's rich coming from the guy who's dated half the women in the damn state." I take a breath and my mind drifts to Devin and that kiss. Thoughts of him have plagued me these past couple of weeks. There's something alluring about someone who doesn't want anything from me. "Maybe I met a guy," I say before I can think better of it.

"Oh, really?" Jake asks.

I lean back. "Yeah. Really. He's a friend of a friend."

"What's this imaginary boyfriend's name?"

"He is neither imaginary nor my boyfriend. Yet. And his name is Devin."

"Holy shit. You're serious!" Jake's eyes go wide and his cider almost comes shooting out of his nose. "Hey, Mom!" he shouts.

I slap a hand over his mouth. "Shut the hell up! Don't you dare tell Mom."

He holds his hands up in surrender. "Must be serious if you don't want Mom finding out about it. 'Cause you know she'll flip, right?"

"God," I groan. "I thought finally being a grandma would satisfy her for a bit."

"Nope. It just kicked her need for grandbabies up to eleven!" Jake jokes.

"You first. I'm not even a real adult yet, remember?"

"Me? You're the one with viable prospects."

I shrug, trying to downplay the unfamiliar warm feeling in my chest when I picture Devin. "Let's not get ahead of ourselves. I barely know him. But there's just something about him."

Jake wraps an arm around my shoulder. "Then go get him, sis." He holds up his cider cup. "To Devin, may he manage the impossible, making Jessica Bridget Allen fall in love."

I elbow him in the ribs and head back out to the ice. *So what if I've never been in love? I'm sure I could fall in love if I wanted to. It's no big deal.*

* * * *

"Come on, Austin," I plead, chasing after him.

"Not happening, Jessie," he answers over his shoulder as he charges through the quad. His pace doubles when he spots Elizabeth. She's staring at the ground and tugging at the straps on her backpack. Her face goes from nervous trepidation to pure joy when she sees the hulking man barreling toward her. He wraps her in a massive bear hug and murmurs something that sounds like "missed you" in her ear before frenching the hell out of her.

They are complete opposites, but they make the cutest couple. Elizabeth and I started off a little rocky. She was wasted the first time we met and nicknamed me Barbie. But I'm not one to hold a grudge. Plus, despite me being tall and blonde, the nickname didn't stick and Elizabeth apologized, so we're good now. She's super sweet and adorably weird.

"Oh, trust me. This is happening. You're just delaying the inevitable." I poke Austin in the shoulder to let him know we aren't done. It's been the same routine for the past month since we got back from Christmas break. I ask for Devin's number and Austin refuses to give it to me.

It's been months since Devin kissed me and I still can't get that brooding jerk out of my head. I'm not the type to obsess over a guy, but he's gotten under my skin. He devastated me with that kiss then just drove off. *Who does that?*

After admitting to Jake how much I liked him, I spent my entire Christmas break scouring social media to find Devin, but the guy is a ghost. He doesn't go to our school and I don't know his last name. All I know is he's a friend of Austin's. Which is why I've resorted to my daily harassment.

"Give me one good reason. I just want his number, not a virgin sacrifice," I deadpan. "Hey, Elizabeth."

"Hey, Jessie," Elizabeth answers with a chuckle. She knows the drill. I badger Austin for eight minutes from the end of our Marketing Principles class until I have to jog across campus to catch my next lecture.

Austin sighs. "Look, I like you, Jessie. But I'm not going to let my best friend be your next conquest."

"Conquest?" I scoff. "I want to date the guy, not plant a 'Jessie was here' flag in his ass."

"You know what I'm talking about. It's a game to you."

"So what if it is? Games are fun, Austin."

"Games are drama. And not Devin's style. So, for the hundredth time, I'm not getting in the middle of this," Austin answers with an exasperated sigh.

"Too late. You introduced us. You're already in the middle."

"What if the situation was reversed? Would you want me giving your number out to strange guys?"

Austin asks. He tucks Elizabeth in against his side and starts walking them towards the parking lot. Elizabeth wraps an arm around his waist and interlaces her fingers with the hand draped over her shoulder. They're sickeningly cute.

I let out a breath. I've never been jealous of someone else's relationship before. I've always known that I want a marriage like my parents', a partnership. But that has always been in the future. The distant, maybe-some-day, can't-really-see-it-from-here future. I've got a lot I want to do before I settle down. Still, having someone look at me the way Austin looks at Elizabeth, like she's his everything, might not be so bad.

"It's not the same thing. I'm not some strange guy. You know me. Devin knows me. He kissed me, for fuck's sake!"

"And yet he still decided not to give you his number. What does that tell you?"

Ouch. Elizabeth comes to a screeching halt. She pulls away from Austin, crosses her arms and glares. She's tiny and about as terrifying as a newborn squirrel, but I'm glad she's on my side.

"Sorry, but it's the truth." Austin holds his arms up in surrender.

"Fine. Then, why don't you give him my number?"

"How do you know I haven't?"

My heart flutters. "Did he ask you for my number?"

"No. He didn't." Austin gives Elizabeth a pointed look. "But he has it. If he hasn't called you, it's because he doesn't want to talk."

"Talking isn't Devin's favorite pastime," Elizabeth adds. "That doesn't mean he isn't interested."

I give her a quick nod. Austin gives her a *WTF* look.

"You have a car, right?" Elizabeth asks, pointing off into the parking lot.

"Yeah, why?"

The mischievous glint in her eyes looks unnatural on Elizabeth's sweet face. "Think it's about time for a service?"

"Elizabeth…" Austin grumbles.

"What? I'm concerned about our friend's safety. Car maintenance is serious." Elizabeth reaches up on her tiptoes and kisses Austin on the cheek before turning to me. "And I happen to know the perfect place."

* * * *

A quick lap of the auto shop parking lot confirms Devin's old muscle car is here. Butterflies dance in my stomach when I open the door to the soft jingle of Christmas bells hanging from the inside handle. Christmas was a few weeks ago, but those bells look like they've been in place for the past dozen Christmases. The faint smell of gas, grime and sweat swirls around me.

The quaint reception area is glassed-in, allowing me to peek out across the garage where guys in overalls are busy on a handful of cars. I examine each one, looking for Devin, but can't see him. There's a young guy, an old guy and a very angry looking woman. I bite my lip as disappointment trickles into my mind.

"Can I help you, Miss?" an older man asks from behind the counter. He has kind blue eyes and a soft smile topped by a thick salt-and-pepper Ron Burgundy-esque mustache. I can't help but smile back.

"Hi, I'm Jessie." I cross the small space and hold out my hand.

"Rob. What can I do for you, Jessie?" he asks, giving my hand a firm shake.

"Well, Rob, I'm looking for a friend of mine who works here. Devin?"

A sly smile curls up the ends of Rob's bushy mustache. He crosses his arms with a light chuckle, nods a few times then calls out, "Devin!"

"What?" a gruff voice hollers from a back room I hadn't noticed before.

"You've got a visitor," Rob adds in a singsong voice. A lesser woman would blush, but I have no shame.

The sound of annoyed grumbling is accompanied by a chair scraping against the floor and paper rustling. I have a meager few seconds to prepare for the sight of Devin's hulking body taking up most of the door frame. He's even sexier than I remember. His tattoos peek out from under a gray shirt whose sleeves are pushed up to his elbows. Over that, he's wearing a dark-blue collared shirt bearing the shop's name on the breast pocket. It's unbuttoned and frames his firm chest. His faded jeans have black stains across the thighs and his feet are clad in scuffed black boots. Combined with the five-o'clock shadow on his strong jaw, his messy black hair and the menacing look in those dark eyes, he belongs on the cover of a sexy workmen's calendar, the kind that has burly half-naked guys in random themes for each month.

Strip him down and hand him a wrench and he could be my Mr. January.

Devin stops dead in his tracks when he sees me. I give him a wave. Rob looks back and forth between the two of us, that mustache twitching with excitement.

"Hey, Devin." I wait for him to respond. To show any sign of recognition. "I'm Austin's friend. Jessie?"

He grunts. *Was that a response? Ugh, this guy's impossible.*

"I brought in the classic I was telling you about." Rob's ears perk up and he leans across the counter, scouring the parking lot.

"2010 Civic," Devin tells Rob flatly. *So he does remember me.*

Rob cracks up laughing. I give a light chuckle. Devin doesn't flinch.

"She's my baby," I deadpan. I level Devin with the sexiest eyes I can muster. "Think you can handle her?"

"What do you need?"

"The full service. Just pop that hood and have at her."

"Keys," he demands.

I toss them at him, underhand but with gusto, aiming for his head. He catches them in his right hand, but moves them to his other and rubs the sting out. He's shaking his head, so I can't be sure, but I'd put money on him fighting back a smile. He brushes past me towards the parking lot. The telltale jingle of those Christmas bells tells me he's through the door. I walk up to Rob, shaking my head.

"I'll tell you what, Rob." I drop onto my elbows on the high counter in front of him. "That is one tough nut to crack."

Rob lets out a jovial chuckle. "He certainly is." Rob leans forward too, matching me.

I narrow my eyes and watch Devin working. He pops the hood and starts poking around at things I don't care to understand.

"Something tells me he's worth it though." I'm talking more to myself than anything.

"For the right woman, I'm sure it is," Rob muses.

I nod a few times, making an impulsive decision that is going to make my busy life just a little bit crazier.

"Okay, Rob. How about you help a girl out?"

Chapter Five

Devin

After five minutes of trying to decipher the chicken scratch on the invoice in front of me, I call out, "Mikey, your handwriting is shit. What did you do on that Ford?"

"The Focus or the Ranger?" he calls.

"Focus."

"Replaced the rear shocks."

That makes more sense than my previous guess of *relays hack*.

The shop is quiet. Instead of managing the counter, I have time for the mind-numbing task of inputting the handwritten invoices from our mechanics into the ancient computer to track our sales and inventory. I hate this shit. I'd much rather be elbow-deep in an engine block, but I've been trapped behind the desk in this cramped back office since Rob had his heart attack two years ago. He's back to working a few days a week now, but I'm still managing pretty much everything. When Rob was in the hospital, I promised his wife, Mandy, I wouldn't let him work himself to death. After everything they've done for me and my sister, it's the least I could do.

I eye the three-inch-high stack of invoices I've still got to go through. I have at least another couple of hours' worth of paperwork, then a couple of hours of wrenching after that. *Looks like it's going to be another long night.* I close my eyes and roll my neck, stretching out some of the stiffness that's settled in.

In the darkness, the image of Jessie's full lips and bright eyes fills the inside of my mind, like they have for the past few weeks since I met the little fireball. She's everything I'm not, filled with unicorns and rainbows and hope. These preppy college girls love the idea of a fling with the bad boy. I've been played by that game before and sure as shit don't need another go.

I have no interest in being her latest hobby. Still, there's no denying Jessie is fucking stunning. I shouldn't have kissed her, but those lips were too delicious to resist. I'm the king of self-control, thanks to a life spent managing the temper I inherited from my asshat father. All that self-control went to shit with the feeling of Jessie pressed against me. I wanted to own her. *Consume her. Keep her.* Even though I knew it'd never happen.

I forced myself to walk away, relieved I'd never see her—or those enticing lips—again. When she showed up at my shop last week looking damn appetizing, I was fucking pissed. She's a temptation I can't afford.

Fucking Austin. Finding the love of his life has made my best friend a matchmaking pain in the ass. I blow out a deep breath and try to focus on the paperwork standing between me and enjoying a beer on my couch.

The jingle of the shop's bell draws my attention away from the Rorschach test that are Mikey's scribbles. I shove back from the desk and stalk to the front. I freeze in the office doorway when I spot a perfect apple-shaped ass in tight jeans bent over behind the counter.

I enjoy the view for longer than a decent guy would, then lick my lips. "Looking for something special?"

Straightening up, she tosses her long blonde hair over her shoulder. She turns, and my chest tightens when I'm blindsided by Jessie's tempting lips curled up in a devious smirk.

When her eyes find mine, an electric current prickles across my skin. Like the first two times I've seen her, I lock down the urge to touch her. *Claim her.*

We share the charged silence for a moment that stretches out into forever. "Aren't we all?"

My pulse kicks up a notch at the sound of her sweet, teasing voice. I ignore it, clenching my jaw and crossing my arms.

"What are you doing here?" I demand, my voice full of vicious disdain.

"I work here," she answers, unfazed.

"No. You don't."

"Yes. I do." She points at the shop's logo over her chest, her smirk widening into a full-blown smug smile. "Rob didn't mention it?"

I shake my head and reach for the phone on the counter. I dial Rob's number from memory, refusing to look at her as the phone rings in my ear.

"Hello?" Rob answers.

"Rob. Devin."

"What's up? There an issue at the shop?"

"Yeah, a stubborn blonde one," I bark.

"Say hello for me," Jessie sings at the same time Rob chuckles on the line.

"She's doing an external business evaluation. For some school project."

I let out a low growl and slide my eyes over Jessie again. She's leaning against the counter, studying me with a hungry curiosity. I leer at her the way an alcoholic does an open bottle of booze.

"I told her you would walk her through the whole operation. Is that a problem?"

"Nothing I can't handle." I hang up without saying goodbye.

Jessie's eyebrows dance and her eyes sparkle. "Where would you like to start?"

I need her out of my space. "Nowhere. Come back next week, when Rob is here. You're his problem."

"Sorry, that's not the deal."

I stare at her until she continues.

"I get to learn the business from *you*." She steps closer, her index finger tracing the shop logo on my shirt. "We're going to get *real* close."

The devil inside me surges forward, desperate for her. I lean down, letting my nose graze her jaw. "And if I refuse?" I drawl. I ignore the way she smells like vanilla and sugar, and how bad I'd like to taste her. *All of her.*

"Rob would be very disappointed. There is another option." She hops up on the counter and crosses her long legs. My gaze traces down them. *Who wears shorts in the middle of winter?* "You ask me out and I'll leave you and your place of work in peace."

"Sounds like blackmail."

"Nope. Blackmail would be if I had a secret I was threatening you with. I'm just offering my services to your boss in a purely professional manner. Unless you want to make our arrangement a personal one —"

"Sexual harassment."

"Sexual harassment would be if I was compelling you to date me in exchange for preferential treatment or professional advancement. This is the exact opposite. Date me and I'll ignore you."

"Fuckin' semantics. Still manipulative bullshit." I hate that she's playing a game, one a part of me would enjoy losing.

"You didn't leave me much choice. I'm just incentivizing the preferred behavior." She grabs a fist full of my shirt and pulls me between her legs. I slap my hands on the counter, my fingers itching to dig into her thighs. Her green eyes lock on me. The tip of her nose nudges mine. "You know there's something here. Why do you keep fighting it? Come on Devin, give in. *Date me.*"

She's a siren, luring me onto the rock, and I can't bring myself to give a fuck. I drag my callused knuckles over the soft skin at her exposed neck, brushing away the silky blonde strands. I take a deep breath, inhaling her sweet smell, and trail a hand down her back. She shudders with a soft hum at my touch, making my cock twitch in my jeans.

She's right about one thing. There is something here. I feel the draw, too. She's temptation incarnate. And no way in hell am I giving in to her. I don't know much about her, but I can tell she's not the type a guy walks away from. She's the type that'll ruin me.

I let myself linger between her thighs and take one last deep breath of her scent before I growl, "That's not happening."

I clasp on her waist, squeezing tighter than needed as I drag her off the counter and shove her away. She gasps at the forcefulness of my rejection. I turn my back on her, ignoring the daggers her eyes are throwing.

"Okay. The hard way it is, Mr. Bennett."

The cheerfulness in her voice is unnerving.

Chapter Six

Jessie

I'm wearing him down. I can feel it. A week in and he's still surly as hell, but he doesn't pull away when I 'accidentally' brush up against him. *Repeatedly.* Rob has kept his end of our secret deal, staying away from the shop and forcing Devin to work with me.

I've never been the girl who chases after a guy. It's not like boys are falling at my feet. Okay, some are. But I've never had to worry about getting a date. Maybe that's why I never tried with any of them — knowing I could have them if I wanted made it not worth the effort. Devin is different. *A challenge.* He's like a drug. I'm addicted to being around him. I've never felt this kind of chemistry before. *This attraction.* He feels it too, even if he refuses to admit it.

We're crammed into the tiny back office, poring over invoices for the millionth hour. The masculine smell of him consumes me. A mix of soap, gasoline and determination—he smells clean but somehow still gritty. The surface may be scrubbed down, but underneath he's all raw manliness.

I shake off the fog of girlish infatuation and stare down at my notebook. The word *dirty* stares back at me. *Don't remember writing that.* I swallow the lump in my throat and scratch out the word rattling around in my subconscious. Devin side-eyes me and I shift in my chair. I flip the page for good measure.

"How many hours a week do you waste trying to read Mikey's handwriting?" I ask, refocusing us on the nonsensical scribble.

He digs the heels of his palms into his eyes. "Too many to count."

I can't help but giggle. He looks up at me with those tired eyes and my cheeks start to flame. I snap my eyes to the blank page in my notebook and write *invoices*.

"And all your invoices are handwritten?" I ask without risking a look up at him.

"Yeah." Devin leans back, the old office chair creaking under his large body. He interlocks his fingers and slides them behind his head. His strong arms and broad chest are like a welcome mat, beckoning me. Jesus, I want to climb into his lap, bury my face in his chest and take a deep breath of Devin's unique smell. I might give it a shot if I thought there was even a small chance he would do anything but push me away and pat me on the head. I've never had a guy be less interested in me than Devin pretends to be. Still, that tic in his jaw makes me think he's not unaffected.

I clear my throat. "You're the only one who inputs the invoices into the computer system?"

"Me or Rob. Mostly me," he answers, staring up at the ceiling tiles like they're more interesting than I am.

"How do you book new appointments?"

"Phone."

"No website? Social media?"

He shakes his head.

"Not even Facebook?"

Another head shake accompanied by an annoyed sigh.

I give him one of my mom's 'ahhh's in response. The simple, judgemental sound conveys so much.

Devin's focus snaps to me as he leans forward, the old chair squealing in objection yet again. *That thing is going to collapse beneath him someday soon.* His stare bores into me, but he doesn't ask me to explain.

I shake my head. "To summarize, you set all appointments, input all invoices into the system, conduct all inventories and manage all scheduling and payroll." I tick off each of his time-consuming jobs on my fingers. His frown deepens with each additional item on the list.

"So?"

"So, what happens when you're not here?"

"I'm always here," he deadpans.

"Always? I bet you're too manly to even get sick, huh? Too tough. The flu knows better than to mess with you, Big Man?"

He looks down at the cement floor to hide his smirk. Seeing that tiny crack in his detached persona sends a shot of heat through my body, like the first sip of whiskey on a cold night. I feel warm and fuzzy. He is adorable and teasing him is my new favorite game. "Ever heard the one about all work and no play?"

He ignores me and turns to the ancient computer on the desk in front of him. *Back to business.* That's my cue to take a tour of the shop, getting to know the people and things that make it tick.

"How long have you worked here?" I ask Sean, doodling on my notebook.

"About fifteen years now I guess," he answers from under the hood of an older Volvo.

"Wow."

Sean's warm chuckle fills the bay where we're talking. His gruff voice and the deep lines around his face give away the years he's spent smoking behind the shop. His long auburn hair is pulled into a ponytail at the nape of his neck. Sean is a sweet old hippie.

My phone buzzes in my pocket. I pull it out to find another missed call from Trevor that I'm too chicken to answer. I've been a flake and I've got a guilt trip coming my way. I bailed on a handful of lectures and two study groups this week. I shoot him a quick text to let him know I'm not going to make it again tonight. I blame my Marketing Principles project, but Devin's the real reason behind my shuffled priorities. I tuck my phone back into my pocket and try to give Sean my undivided attention.

"Seems like most of you guys have been around for a minute. Guess Rob is a pretty good boss, then."

"Rob is good people," Sean answers without hesitation. "Never known someone with a heart that big. Him and Mandy both."

The more I talk to the people in this little shop, the more I realize it's a family as much as it's a business. These people know one another. *Love one another.*

"I'm surprised he's not here more often," I muse.

Sean stops wrenching on whatever he's got going on under that hood and leans against the bumper. "He gave us a scare a couple years back. Mandy made him promise to take it easy after the heart attack."

My pen stills. Concern flits across Sean's face.

"Thought we were gonna lose him." Sean nods to the front office, where Devin is helping a customer. "Dev kept us going. Not sure what would've happened to the shop without him."

I watch Devin through the glass. *That explains why he takes so much on his shoulders.* I nod and Sean returns to his work under the hood.

I wander to the next bay, catching the eye of a guy about my age working on a car older than both of us. He's cute, with bright blue eyes and sandy-blond hair sticking out of his backwards baseball cap. He has a chill surfer vibe.

He greets me with a "Sup."

"Hey. I'm Jessie." I give him a quick wave.

"I'm Mikey. You're the one Rob said was going to be doing some business evaluation or something?"

I nod. "Yep. That's me."

Mikey looks me up and down. "He didn't say you'd be so hot."

Ignoring his flirting, I pick up the invoice sitting on the tool bench in front of me and squint at the gibberish.

"What are you working on today?"

"Serpentine belt replacement."

I shake my head. There is no way the jumble of swirls and loops on this paper says anything resembling that. "Are you left-handed?"

"No," he answers. A blush creeps up his neck and he goes back to tinkering under the hood of the car.

I smile and hold up the invoice. "You sure? Might be worth giving it a shot."

Mikey's forced laugh echoes off the engine block. "Not you too. Devin's always giving me shit for my handwriting. I'm a mechanic, not a calligrapher."

"Fair enough." I can't help but wonder. "This might sound like a weird question, but would you mind writing something down for me?"

"Ugh—" Mikey scratches hard at the skin on his forearm.

I place my hand over his fresh trail of red marks. "Please?" I ask again, soft and sweet.

"Sure. I guess," he relents with a sigh.

I hand him my notebook and Mikey grips the pen between his index and middle finger, guiding it with all five fingers. He stares at the blank page, his eyes blinking rapidly and a small bead of sweat appearing at his temple.

"There are eight carburetors in inventory," I dictate. Mikey's hand doesn't move. He swallows hard. Slow and clear, I repeat, "There are eight carburetors in inventory."

"This is stupid," he mutters, shoving my notebook at me. "I've got work to do. Devin will have my ass if he sees me wasting time on some stupid..." He trails off, shame and vulnerability choking his words.

I step in closer, lowering my voice. "Have you ever been tested for dyslexia?"

"No. I'm not stupid or anything," he snaps.

I bite the inside of my mouth to avoid cussing him out. "It has nothing to do with intelligence. It just means your brain is wired different. My brother is dyslexic. And he's one of the smartest people I know."

Mikey crumples forward, his chin dropping to his chest. "Sorry, I didn't mean—"

"How the fuck are we out of spark plugs?" an angry woman's voice calls out across the shop.

The source of the voice is a woman in her forties who looks like Rosie the Riveter after some jail time. Her bright red lipstick matches the red bandana that's holding back her pitch-black hair. Short bangs and an eyebrow ring frame the deep worry lines on her forehead. A tattoo that looks like the green tail of a dragon peeks out of her massive cleavage. *I have to ask her where she got that push-up bra. It defies gravity!*

She rushes past Mikey and me, storming straight to the office. "Devin!" she screeches the whole way there.

I give Mikey a forgiving nod and I back away. "Oh, I've got to see this."

Prison Rosie throws the door open and it clangs against the wall with an echoing thud. I sneak in behind her and hug the wall. Devin slices his eyes to her, pinning her in place with a vicious silent warning.

"Wait," he growls, a low and guttural sound. The strength in that single word has both me and Prison Rosie frozen in place.

Devin returns his attention to his customer, a lady who must be in her seventies trying to pay with a check. He is patient, his voice now a gentle soothing drawl. "Thank you for your business, ma'am. Drive safe." Devin hands her the keys to her Ford Falcon. She waves goodbye and heads out to the car almost as old as she is.

Before the jingle of the doorbell fades, Devin's furious gaze is back on the woman mechanic. "What?" he barks.

"We're out of M14 spark plugs." She huffs.

While the two are locked in a staring contest for the ages, I slip behind the counter.

"Spark plugs," the woman repeats, throwing her arms up.

"I heard you, Shelley."

Shelley — AKA Prison Rosie — scoffs and storms off, muttering obscenities I've never heard before on her return journey to her bay.

I inch into Devin's personal space, lean against the counter and stare up at him. He doesn't look at me, doesn't flinch, pretending I don't exist. I resist the urge to pinch his butt just to get a reaction out of him. I hop up onto the counter, knowing it annoys him, and cross my legs.

"That was kinda hot," I tease.

A soft rumble of his chest is the only indication he heard me. "You can stop with the statue impersonation, Big Man. I know you can talk." I poke him in the shoulder.

He grabs my waist to pull me off the counter. I lean back and grab the edge behind me. I'm not going to make it easy on him. His callused fingers slide around my wrists with a firm grip and I lose my hold. Pinning my arms behind my back, Devin slides me off and into him. My chest is pressed against his. His eyes are burning into me. My heart is doing its best to smash through my rib cage and my mouth is drier than the Gobi Desert.

"I'm not sure which one is sexier, Sweet Devin or Angry Devin." I hum, my body charged under his electric touch. He tightens his grip on my wrists, pulling me harder against him as he leans down. My eyes flutter closed and my lips part to suck in a ragged breath.

The doorbell jingles and Devin's body shoots away from mine. Frustration surges through me and I whip around to meet the unwelcome intruder.

"Am I interrupting something?" a cute girl asks from the doorway with a mischievous smirk. She can't be much more than sixteen or seventeen, but the way Devin clears his throat and reorganizes a stack of invoices, you'd think we'd just been caught butt-naked and going at it. *Holy shit, is he blushing?* Too adorable for words.

I slap on my customer-service face. "Welcome to East Side Auto Service. How can we help you?"

The girl looks between Devin and me. Devin's ignoring her. I'm grinning like an idiot. She takes a couple of tentative steps forward. "And you are?"

"Jessica Allen." Feeling the tension rolling off Devin beside me, I can't help but add, "Devin's future girlfriend. And you are?"

Devin's eyes snap to me and, without looking, I feel them searing the side of my face.

The girl looks back at Devin and cracks up. She closes the distance to the counter. "Rebecca Bennett. Devin's sister."

I shake her hand and we both send teasing glances over to Devin. He groans and the sound makes me want to push him further. I slide around the counter and wrap Rebecca in a hug. She goes with it, loving the irritation splashed across her brother's face as much as me.

"Sister!" I exclaim. "I've always wanted a little sister." Rebecca and I both laugh.

Devin snaps, "What do you need, Becs?"

"Me? I'm just here to get to know my future sister-in-law," she deadpans.

Devin scoffs and skulks off to the back office.

Becs holds up her hand for a high-five. *I think I love her.*

Chapter Seven

Jessie

I am nervous. I know the business plan I've laid out for the shop is solid. I've spent almost every free waking minute on this thing. It's not convincing Rob I'm worried about. It's Devin. If his veiled antagonism is anything to go off, he's going to resist my ideas like his life depends on it.

I take a sip of my salted caramel latte and try to calm the hornets' nest in my stomach. I asked Rob and Devin to meet me at the coffee house down the street from the shop. The three of us weren't going to fit in that tiny office without me sitting in Devin's lap. *On second thought, that might not have been so bad.* I look down at the papers I have spread out on the table and push aside the rogue thought. This is business. As much as I want to steal more time with Devin, this plan is about more than that. I think it can make a difference.

The door to the coffee house opens and I look up. The sight of Rob striding towards me with a warm smile under that bushy mustache eases my nerves. We don't know each other that well, but he wraps me in a warm hug regardless. Over the past few weeks, I've come to care about his little shop and everyone in it.

My gaze shifts to Devin and my breath catches. He reaches out his hand, trailing his fingers along the inside of my palm before encasing it in a firm shake. His soft touch shocks me. *How can a handshake be erotic?* Heat surges up my arm and across my body as I stare into his dark eyes. I've never wanted to put my lips on someone so bad in my life.

"I'm ready to hear all these brilliant ideas of yours." Rob clears his throat next to us, reminding me we're in public and I shouldn't mount Devin like a wild animal in heat.

I drop his hand like it's a live wire and take a deep breath. *Here we go.* I launch into my professional business proposal.

"First of all, Rob, let me commend you" — I slide my gaze to Devin — "both of you, on creating a phenomenal team. Spending time in your shop made it clear that it's more than a business. It's a family." Rob nods. Devin grunts. I've spent enough time with him to know this one is his approval grunt. It's shorter than his annoyed sigh and higher pitched than his pissed-off groan.

"I don't want to change that. But there are a few ways we could improve. My plan focuses on two primary areas. First, transitioning to computerized booking and invoicing. Then, building a social media platform to increase your customer base." This time Devin gives me both his sigh and his groan. *Great.* Rob puts on his glasses and examines the charts I've laid out.

Devin doesn't bother looking over the numbers I've spent hours creating. "Business is good. Shop's busy," he declares.

"You have a solid customer base right *now*, but you're not growing. And, to be honest, your current customers are getting to the age where they aren't going to be driving much longer." In the dozen or so hours I've spent in the shop over the past two weeks, I haven't seen a single customer who doesn't qualify for the early-bird special.

"Nothing wrong with new customers. Everyone is online now," Rob says, playing peacemaker. He gives Devin a stern, disappointed look. I try—and fail—not to look smug. "I can't get that sister of yours to put down her cell phone for more than five minutes. Damn thing is practically glued to her hand." I look between Rob and Devin, confused. Rob makes it sound like he's more than just Devin's boss. *Stepdad maybe?* "Tell me about this new computer system."

I perk up, excited about this system and how much easier it's going to make Devin's life. "I researched a wide variety of systems, all with a different array of functionality, to find the ideal one to address your shop's specific needs while maintaining a low price point."

I open my laptop, loading the software interface for a demonstration. I click through a few menus. "It is clean and simple, easy to use but has all the functions your staff will need to replace your current paper system." I pull a box of brake pads out of my bag and open the app on my phone. "Any smart phone or device can be turned into an inventory scanner." I hold my phone over the barcode and wait for the beep before pointing to the screen.

"Would you look at that?" Rob grins when the brake pads pop up on the new invoice.

I smile wide, ignoring Devin's gaze. "Each part will be added to an invoice automatically when scanned by your mechanic and simultaneously removed from inventory. This system will manage inventory, payroll, billing and scheduling. It even has interoperability to facilitate online customer bookings."

Rob nods in approval. Devin scowls at me.

"Best of all, no more hours wasted with redundant data entry or trying to read Mikey's horrible chicken scratch."

Rob chuckles.

"We can't afford this," Devin snaps.

I grit my teeth and resist the overpowering urge to snarl. "While there will be upfront costs, these technological improvements will grow your customer base while streamlining overhead and minimizing non-income-generating man hours. As far as training is concerned, I've selected a program that's intuitive to minimize training time."

"The guys are never going to figure out how to use it. Waste of money," Devin argues.

I rest my elbows on the table, lean forward, and narrow my eyes on Devin. "You could at least pretend to keep an open mind. Not all change is bad."

"Not everything needs to be fixed."

"You don't give us old dogs enough credit, Dev. Some of us like learning new tricks," Rob butts in.

"Thank you, Rob." Devin and I both lean back and cross our arms. Rob studies the charts in front of him while we leer at each other. There is a challenge in

Devin's eyes. His glares at me like he wants me and hates me a little because of it.

"I'm going to have to talk it over with Mandy." Rob re-stacks the charts in a neat pile. "How about you two come over for dinner tomorrow night?" he asks, standing. Devin and I don't break eye contact as we both get up and push our chairs in.

"I'd love to." Syrup coats my words and I glare at Devin.

He grunts in the affirmative.

Sounds like we've got a date.

* * * *

Okay, so not a date. More like I'm crashing a family dinner.

"Come in, darling. Come in. Come in!" Mandy, Rob's wife, tells me as I stand awkwardly in their entryway. She waves me forward and pulls me into a full-contact hug once I'm in arm's reach. She rocks me back and forth, reminding me of my grandmother. Grannie Allen hugs me like I've just returned from the edge of the world after years of toiling to save the human race. Grannie's arms wrap me in love. And so do Mandy's.

"We're huggers," she explains when she lets me go. "I'm Mandy Reece. Rob's better half."

"And she doesn't let me forget it either," Rob teases behind her. Without looking, Mandy smacks him on the shoulder.

"Jessie!" Rebecca calls from the top of the stairs, jogging down to greet me.

"Rebecca!" I call.

"Urgh. I hate Rebecca. Everyone calls me Becs." She slides in between me and Mandy, wrapping me in a hug. "We're huggers."

"So I've been warned." I hug her in return, picking her up and shaking her like a ragdoll. *When in Rome.* I set her down again and look at her. She's a beautiful young woman. She has Devin's same olive skin and dark hair, but her eyes are a lighter hazel color. She's just as striking, but softer and more feminine than her brother. *She'll be a little heartbreaker, no doubt.* "Becs Bennett? How alliterative. Tell me, BeeBee" — I pause to let her take in her new nickname — "did your brother bring you so that I'd go easy on him?"

A growl from the end of the hall alerts me to Devin's presence. My heart drops into my stomach so it has more room to do its compulsory happy dance. He's leaning against the doorjamb, arms crossed and a small scowl on those beautiful lips. He's cleaned up in a button-down shirt and dark jeans. His face is clean-shaven and his hair is freshly washed and slicked back. My fingers itch to mess it up.

Still tucked into my side, Becs giggles. "Nah. I live here. Rob and Mandy adopted me forever and a day ago. Dev didn't tell you?"

That explains why Rob talked about her as though she was his daughter, because she *is* his daughter. The shop is one big family and they've welcomed me with open arms. The realization warms my chest. I resist the urge to ask what happened to her parents. *Their parents.*

"*Dev* isn't much of a talker. He's the strong silent type."

Becs slides out from under my arm and prowls up to her brother. "I wish. Big brother lives to lecture me!"

She pokes him in the side and he curls forward with an exaggerated howl.

"When you need it." He gives her a gentle shove on her shoulder. She sticks her tongue out at him. They're sweet together. I love the playful side of Devin Bennett. He catches me staring, my eyes no doubt wide with giddy delight, and nods. "We eatin' or what?"

"Once you come greet our guest like the gentleman I know you are," Mandy scolds.

Devin shoves off the wall and stalks over to me, his eyes full of an intimidating hunger. I swallow hard, my throat tight. He sets a strong hand on my waist and leans in. The familiar smell of citrus and man fills my senses. I bite back a moan. He places a chaste kiss on my cheek that curls my toes.

"Welcome," he murmurs in my ear and my knees go weak. One word and I'm a puddle for this man. I'd be ashamed of myself if I was capable of any emotion other than desire. Devin pulls away and peers down at me with those coal-black eyes and a lopsided grin. *Holy hell, it's indecent for him to be so damn sexy in front of his family.*

Rob clears his throat next to me. I shake my head and turn to see the three of them staring at me and Devin. I realize I have a handful of Devin's shirt in my greedy fist and I'm biting my bottom lip. Rob looks amused, Mandy scandalized and Becs mischievous. I let go of Devin's shirt and flatten out the wrinkles with both hands while I avoid eye contact with everyone.

"Let's go," Rob announces as he pulls Mandy and Becs into the dining room.

Devin and I are alone in the entryway. He slaps his hand over mine to still my fiddling with his shirt. I drop my head to his chest and let out a deep exhale.

"You're killin' me, Big Man," I mumble to his chest pocket.

"Right back at you, JB." I can't tell if he's amused or annoyed. Maybe both. I pull my head up and stare at him. He's trying to look distant and angry, scowl locked in place. But those eyes give him away. They're smoldering for me and I can't help but smile at the sight. He nods behind us.

"Right. Let's do this," I chirp, extracting myself from Devin and strolling into the dining room as if I wasn't seconds from mauling him in his family's entryway. I can control myself. I hope.

I follow Jessie into the dining room, showing monk-like restraint in not staring at her perfect ass. That soft moan she let out in front of everyone just about killed me. My fingers itch to touch this woman, no matter who's watching. I sit down at the table and cross my arms, locking down my wandering fingers. Mandy has Jessie sitting next to me and the last thing I need is to find my hand on her thigh halfway through Meatloaf Monday.

"So how did you two meet?" Mandy asks Jessie.

"Party —"

"At a campus party —" Jessie and I start talking at the same time. I'm done explaining, but she keeps going. "We have a mutual friend on the football team, so we were both at this afterparty. I saw him from across the room and that was that." She side-eyes me with a smirk.

"Love at first sight? How sweet!" Mandy coos, clasping a hand over her heart.

I shake my head and say, "We're not together."

"Yet," Jessie adds with a suggestive wiggle of her eyebrows.

Mandy shakes her head. "I thought you said Devin was bringing his girlfriend for dinner?" she asks Becs.

"No, I said he's bringing his *future* girlfriend." Becs winks at Jessie, who gives her a high-five across the table.

"Bet your ass, sister," Jessie adds, and I have to choke back a laugh. *The balls on this woman.* "Oh, sorry, Mandy. My mom'd skin me alive if she heard me cuss at the dinner table."

"Then I guess we shouldn't tell her," Mandy answers. "So, what does it mean to be Devin's future girlfriend?"

Jessie steeples her fingers in front of her and squints. "Right now, it consists mostly of growls, grunts and frustration."

"So just like being his *actual* girlfriend!" Becs titters.

"Enough," I howl.

Rob takes pity on me and changes the subject. "She's put a lot of effort into developing those plans for the shop I showed you."

Mandy sets her hand on top of Jessie's. "Thank you so much for that, dear. You don't know how worried I am about him going back to work these days. All that stress and those long hours." Mandy gets a bit choked up and I stare down at my meatloaf.

"This system should help with both of those." Jessie squeezes Mandy's hand and smiles.

"If it works," I hear myself add before I can stop it.

Jessie turns to glare at me and Mandy's lips slip into a pout.

"Why wouldn't it work?" Mandy asks.

"Don't listen to him," Jessie reassures her. "Devin thinks all change is bound to lead to disaster. He'd still be chiseling invoices into cave walls if he had his way."

Becs snorts and I shoot her a warning glare. She sticks her tongue out at me. *I get no respect in this house.*

"It's complicated. We're simple. Won't work," I answer.

"More complicated than rebuilding an engine?" Jessie quips. *Touché.*

"That's different."

"No. It's not, Negative Nancy. It just takes dedication and persistence. Two things I happen to excel at." I can't help but think she's talking about something else. "I can be just as stubborn as you."

"It's a risk. An expensive one."

"And worth it. You've gotta risk it for the biscuit. Gotta spend money to make money."

Rob hums at my side and I know I'm fighting a losing battle.

"I've thought about it quite a bit, and I think we're worth the investment," Rob declares. I grumble. Jessie squeals. "If the projections are even half as good as Jessie thinks they will be, it'll be worth it. Plus, it might free up some of your evenings, Dev."

I focus on eating my dinner as fast as possible. The last thing I need in my life right now is Jessica Allen. She's perky and optimistic and idealistic. All the things I'm not.

If I'm not careful, she'll convince me there's a future here. But there isn't. Not with her. She'll have her fun and move on. I'm not volunteering to be her pet project, no matter how perfect her body is or how her smile makes me desperate to kiss her.

Chapter Eight

Devin

"No," I bark at her, knowing I'll be ignored. It's been like this all week. She flies around changing shit. Moving shit. *Improving* shit. I like things the way they are. My way. The only thing that needs changing is her in my space, the smell of her sugary skin begging to be licked.

"Yes. Yes. Yes."

Now my dick is hard.

Fuck.

I snatch the paint swatches out of her hands and toss them into the trash as I stalk off across the shop. Putting the counter between us, I growl, "I don't need new paint."

"For the ninth time, yes *we* do." She gestures around the small shop, pointing at our crimson walls.

"I painted last year."

A mischievous little smirk appears on her full lips, making me think it turns her on to piss me off. "I appreciate that. And while I love the red" — she saunters up to the trash can and plucks the paint samples out of the abyss — "blue is the best color for a small business. Especially one where people already think you're trying to rip them off."

"Says who?"

"About a million marketing experts and the few thousand psychologists they paid to figure it out." She puckers those rosy lips and blows this morning's coffee grounds off her multi-colored swatches. My dick twitches despite my frustration. Every damn thing this woman does gets under my skin.

"Blue promotes calm, stability and trust."

"And red?" I can't keep myself from asking.

"You picked it, didn't you?" I nod and she nibbles at her bottom lip. "Red means passion, urgency. *Hunger*," she says on a ragged breath.

I grab a clipboard off the wall and look over today's schedule. She giggles from right behind me.

Her phone buzzes for the millionth time today. She lets out a sad sigh, types something out and tucks it back into her pocket. The damn thing is always going off and it never seems to do anything but drive her nuts. I'd tell her to just turn the damn thing off it were any of my business. But it's not. She can torture herself all she wants.

I'm pretending to scan the list of appointments in front of me when her accusing voice asks, "Why are you still using a handwritten schedule? I've already input all the appointments into the new computer system."

The overpriced thing she talked Rob into buying was set up a few days ago, but I refuse to touch it. I don't need it. *Don't want it.*

"Because I trust *my* schedule more than some system. Despite it not being blue."

My skin prickles when she puts a hand on my forearm. My sleeves are pushed up to my elbows, like always, and the skin-to-skin touch distracts me long enough for her to pluck the clipboard out of my hands. She's running a finger down the list and walking backward.

I groan and chase after her. Without looking up, she sidesteps and dodges my searching hands. We dance around the small shop, me lumbering after her and her gliding just out of reach like a seasoned boxer. *Fuck, she's slippery.*

Every time she evades my clutches, the corners of her lips curve up. Her gaze snaps to the bays, searching behind me where everyone is busy working. And I'm in here playing keep-away with a co-ed. I manage to corner her, but she slides the clipboard behind her back. She let me catch her. I reach around her and grab her wrist. I'm forceful, but she resists. She's deceptively strong and all I manage to do is pull her body against mine.

She runs hot and her skin burns into mine through our clothes. My head tells me to step back, but I am too stubborn to let her win this little game. I peer down at her. I've made men piss their pants with this look, but Jessie just smiles up at me, happy as a pig in shit.

"You know why that's funny?" she asks, cocking an eyebrow.

"Why?" I ask, my voice huskier than I'd like.

In one swift motion she shoves the clipboard into my chest and steps back. "Your schedule is wrong."

I'm searching the list, checking it against the cars out in the service bays. Jessie skips —*fucking skips*— over to the counter, clicks a couple of buttons on the computer and prints out a new schedule.

She slaps the paper down in front of me, pointing to the yellow highlighted Buick that isn't on my schedule.

"The guy with the F-150 canceled, so an internet appointment was slated in its place about an hour ago. Better keep up, Big Man."

I toss the clipboard down on the counter and retreat to the office. I sit down in my ancient office chair and start poring over yesterday's invoices. Her system is supposed to handle all the invoices and inventory too, but for now I was able to convince Rob to keep up the paper system that's always worked. She can try her experiment, and when it fails and she leaves, I'll still keep us going.

Jessie props that perfect ass against the desk beside me, her hip brushing against my forearm. I don't move. *Don't react.* I'm not giving in to her. She's done pushing my buttons.

She waves the paint swatches in front of my face. "I'm thinking I can take Mikey to pick up the paint with me tomorrow afternoon and we can paint after we close. It's a small enough space. It should only take a few hours."

I give her a low hum in acceptance. She swings away, tucks the samples into her back pocket and saunters out of the door.

"Change is good, Big Man. You're gonna like it. I promise," she sings from the front of the shop.

Doorbells jingle and I let out a deep sigh, knowing she's gone.

I drag a hand down my face and let out a low laugh. *No, JB. I'm not going to like it. Being around you is torture.*

Chapter Nine

Devin

"How 'bout you dial it back a notch," Austin complains, shaking out his padding-coated hand.

I don't listen as I pummel the focus mitts he holds up in front of me, my glove hitting with a satisfying *thwack*. I've got too much pent-up energy to take it easy on him. He makes it another five minutes before he bows out. I transition to the heavy bag, and Austin slides in behind the bag and holds it steady.

"What's got you so worked up, Big Man?" He uses Jessie's stupid nickname and laughs. The fucker *laughs*. I hit the bag hard enough to knock him back a few steps. "She's getting under your skin, huh?"

He's got that stupid smirk on his face. I fantasize about punching his teeth out. Maybe hitting my best friend will release some of this tension, because destroying this damn punching bag isn't doing shit.

I pull off the gloves and let out a long groan. "This is your fault, asshole."

"Oh no, I can't take credit for you being so damn irresistible." He licks his lips and eye-fucks me like a depraved pervert. "You know you're delicious man candy."

He's impossible sometimes. Everything is a joke to Austin, including my torture at the hands of a sexy, sadistic co-ed. I shove the gloves into my bag and head towards the door.

"Hey, wait up." Austin chases after me. We walk next to each other silently, until we make it to my car. I toss the gym bag into my passenger seat and slam the door closed.

Austin runs his hands through his golden locks and gets serious for half a second. "Dude, I kept my mouth shut. It was Elizabeth. She seems to think you and Jessie would be good together."

I like Elizabeth. She's good for him. The weird little geek keeps him focused on not fucking up his life. He needs that—a purpose. I don't. I know who I am and I've got everything I need. Elizabeth playing matchmaker and wreaking havoc on my life pisses me off.

"If you could keep your girlfriend out of my business, that'd be fucking fantastic."

"That woman knows a thing or two about how to love. Plus, she's smarter than both of us combined. Maybe she has a point." He laughs. In only a few months, he went from serial player to lovestruck dipshit. It's obvious he's totally gone, beyond in love with her. "Besides, the damage seems like it's already been done."

"Don't I know it."

"It can't be that bad. Having something a little nicer to look at than greasy dudes. Or is that your thing?" Austin winks.

"Fuck off." I wipe my hand down my face, trying to erase the image of Jessie's bright smile. "You have no idea. She's everywhere, man. Getting into everything."

"And you want to get into her?" Austin deadpans.

I ignore him and walk around the hood to the driver's-side door. Austin follows after me, laughing lightly.

"Sorry, couldn't help myself. You walked into that one." He grabs my door so I can't slam it in his face. "So, why don't you? We both know you've wanted her since that party."

"She's not my style."

Austin cocks his head to the side and stares at me. The shape of Jessie's curves flash through my mind again and I know I'm full of shit. She's gorgeous. She's every man's style. That's the problem. A girl like that has options. A future. Somewhere far away from my dirty little auto shop. Any fun we might have isn't going to beyond a few months. I'm sure the fireworks would be spectacular right until they burn my life to ash. The drama ain't worth it. I like steady. *Reliable.*

"It's not going to hurt anything to have a little fun for once, Dev." Austin lets go of the door and slaps the hood of my car. "Who knows, you might like it."

I rev the engine as I drive off. *Fuck Austin. Fuck Jessie. Fuck everyone trying to tell me what I'm going to like.*

I lock myself in my office after the gym and charge through the day, forgetting Austin and all the rest of it. The door jingles and the sound of Jessie's light laugh fills the shop. It's an amazing sound, like pure unadulterated happiness. Like nothing in life could ever touch her. It grates on my nerves for reasons I'm not willing to admit. I walk to the office doorway and take in the sight of Mikey making goofball faces at Jessie, who's doubled over in laughter.

"I swear, he blew up like a marshmallow over the fire!" He sets down the large paint cans he's holding and floats around the shop like he's a balloon in the Macy's day parade, arms wide and cheeks puffed out. He catches me staring. Straightening up, he clears his throat and looks sheepishly back at Jessie. "Hey, Dev. I was just telling Jessie about that time Sean forgot he was allergic to shellfish."

"How does someone forget they're allergic to something?" She giggles, setting down two large bags full of what looks like painting supplies. She turns to face me, tracing her gaze up my body, her eyes sparkling with delight when they meet mine.

I'm snarling and she's smiling. *This woman doesn't intimidate easily. She'd laugh in Death's face.*

"That's Sean for you," Mikey adds. I glare at him and he wipes his sweaty palms on his jeans. "I'll just go see if anyone needs help cleaning up." He slips out to the service bays, leaving me alone with Jessie.

"Have fun?" I bark out.

She looks over at where Mikey's stealing glances at her. "Sure. He's sweet."

It bothers me even though I know it shouldn't. She can flirt with whoever the hell she wants. I stalk up to her, encroaching on her personal space. She doesn't budge. She straightens up and pulls her shoulders back.

"Can I help you with something, Big Man?" she asks, staring up at me,

I nod down to the bags.

"I got a handful of brushes, some drop cloths and some painter's tape. Just the basics."

I grunt in approval, focused more on the heat radiating off her body and the vanilla smell of her than her words. Her hair is up in the same ponytail as always, but a wisp has slipped out. I want to roll the strands between my fingers, feel their softness under my fingertips as I lift them to my nose and take a deep inhale.

She's off in a flash, buzzing around the room, rambling about all the prep work she's going to get done before we close in twenty minutes. I watch her scurry around and hum. *She's got nervous energy to burn. Maybe I should have taken her to the gym instead of Austin this morning.*

I slip into the office and let the Jessie tornado tear through the shop. By the time I come out half an hour later, she's got everything off the walls and all the furniture pushed into the middle of the space, covered in a drop cloth. She's up on a ladder, laser focused on painting a straight line along our ceiling. Mikey's underneath her, laser focused on her exposed thighs.

"How's it look?" she calls down to him.

"Great," he coos.

Fuck this.

In three large steps I'm across the shop, gripping Mikey's shoulder and squeezing hard. He backs away, arms raised in surrender. He grabs his jacket off the pile in the middle of the room and heads for the door without turning his back on me.

"Hey, where are you going?" Jessie asks when she hears the door chime.

"Sorry, Jess, I gotta head out. Forgot I've g-got some p-plans for dinner," he stammers. Mikey's always been a bit of a pussy.

She looks down at me, her eyebrows pinched together. "What was that about?"

I don't answer. My eyes are locked on the skirt tucked under her as she sits on the top rung of the ladder. It's riding high on her thigh, showing off those legs that seem to go on forever. I don't bother answering her. Instead, I grip her waist and pull her down, keeping my eyes focused on the floor beneath us until her feet come into view. Her shirt slips up and my right hand slides against her silky skin. I'm staring at it, the spot where my skin is melting into hers.

"Hey!" she shouts.

The paintbrush in her hand tickles my cheek and she presses into my chest. I tighten my grip on her waist and my fingers ache to slip farther under her shirt. She looks up at me and our eyes lock. My heart skids to a stop in my chest. Her eyes are so green, turbulent like the ocean during a storm.

"Hey," she murmurs in my arms. I'm leaning down, giving in to whatever draw she has on me. I brush my nose against her hair and take a deep breath, inhaling her sweetness. She moans in my ear. Her eyes flutter shut and her mouth falls open the smallest bit. I lick my lips, hovering just above hers. I'm desperate to know if all of her tastes as sweet as she smells.

The shop phone rings and I snap back to reality. I shove her away, turning and striding into the office as fast as I can without looking like I'm running.

"*Hey!*" she shouts at my retreating back. Those three letters manage to carry an unnerving amount of anger and frustration. She follows me and slams the office door behind her even though we're the only ones here.

"East Side Auto?" I say into the receiver. A guy's voice rambles into my ear, but I can't comprehend his words.

"Hey," she shouts again from across the small space. I hold up a finger and point to the phone. "Oh hell no. I don't care if that is the *Pope!* Hang up the damn phone and get back over here."

I lean on the edge of the desk. "Uh huh," I say to the guy, who's mimicking the high-pitched squealing sound of what I'm guessing is a loose fan belt.

Jessie rips the phone out of my hand. "I'm sorry, but we're closed." She slams the phone down and grabs my shirt. My knuckles go white when I grip the edge of the desk to keep myself from touching her. I could take her right here, in this office. A quick swipe to send invoices and shit tumbling to the floor and I could prop that sexy ass on the desk and...*fuck.*

"You scared off my help," she accuses, her voice hoarse and her chest heaving.

"He scares easy."

"Listen to me, Devin Bennett. I already have *three* overly protective brothers. I. Do. Not. Need. A. Fourth." She steps between my spread thighs, pressing her chest against mine. "Now, if you want to talk about becoming my jealous boyfriend —"

"Not happening."

She releases my shirt and pats my chest. She spins around, whipping me in the face with that damn ponytail. My dick stirs. *Now hairplay is my fetish?*

She's halfway to the door. "Then you'll just have to get used to anyone looking at me however and whenever they want."

"Don't wear skirts on ladders," I command.

She pauses in front of the door with her back to me, bends forward a few inches, lifts up her skirt and flashes me her bright red panties. Turning, she rests her chin on her shoulder with a sinister grin.

"I'm wearing boy shorts," she says as if that makes a difference. She drops her skirt, but it's too late. The vision of her perfect ass in those red panties is burned into my memory forever.

I cross the room and slam the door shut when she tries to open it. I press my body against hers and cage her in.

Her voice cracks. "It's killing you, isn't it? Losing control."

"My shop. My rules."

"My body. My rules." She shifts her hips against me. I wrap an arm around her waist and hold her there. "You've made it quite clear that *my* business is none of *your* business."

"What will it take to make you behave?"

"Date me," she answers, triumph in her voice.

"No," I growl.

"Yes," she moans.

I drop my forehead to her shoulder and fill my senses with her. She'll consume every inch of me. "One date."

"Three," she counters.

"Two."

"Three. Final offer, or next time I'll go commando." Her voice is sultry. Her tight ass pressed against me makes it impossible to hide how hard I am.

"Three." My voice is the angry low rumble of an eight-cylinder diesel.

She twirls in my arms like the tornado she is, a bright smile on her beautiful, innocent face. She kisses me on the cheek, shoves me back and slips out of the door.

"Good. Now, get out here and help me paint."

What the fuck *just happened?*

Chapter Ten

Devin

I take a long pull on my beer and try to figure out how the hell I got here. I look at my hands wrapped around the neck of the bottle. They're rough, callused and stained with black grime. I spent thirty minutes scrubbing my fingernails, using half a damn bottle of orange degreaser. My fingers are raw and there's still a coat of dirt that just won't go away. I run my fingers through my hair and take a deep breath. Jessie wants this. She thinks she wants me. She doesn't even know me. She will by the end of the night.

For our first 'date' I told her to meet me at a nasty dive bar. It's dark and dank, smelling like old sweat and fresh bodily fluids. My boots stick to the floor from what I'm hoping is spilled beer. *Little Miss Sunshine is going to have a rude awakening tonight.*

I'm sitting at the far end of the L-shaped bar, facing the door. I spot her the second she walks in. She's drop-dead gorgeous. Sexy heels, tight black pants, flowing top that skirts the swell of her breasts. My dick stirs in my pants and I let out a possessive growl. She should not be dressed like that here. A dozen sets of sleazy eyes peruse her figure as she stands in the doorway. She bites her lip, searching the room for me. I raise my hand, but she doesn't see me tucked in the corner.

I stand and cross the bar to her, pushing a few gawking assholes out of my way with more force than needed. The second her gaze lands on me, relief washes over her face, followed by a quick blush and a wide grin. She is so fucking beautiful when she smiles.

"Hi!" she calls out. I don't answer. I step into her, wrap an arm around her waist and pull her against me. Her body is a thousand degrees and it burns into mine. She puts a hand on my chest, just above my heart. I swear, the stupid thing tries to break through my chest and jump into her palm.

I lean into her. "It's dangerous looking like that in a place like this."

"Careful, that almost sounded like a compliment." She nuzzles against my jaw. "Good thing you're here to protect me, Big Man."

I guide her to the corner, keeping a possessive hand on her back and glaring daggers at anyone who looks at her, which is everyone with a dick and a few without.

"What are you drinking?" she asks.

I sink down onto my bar stool and hold up my beer. She snatches it out of my hand and takes a sip.

"Mmmm. Yummy." She licks her lips and I'm mesmerized. Those lips are pure torture. They hitch up on one side while I stare at them and I know she's laughing at me. "Thanks."

This crazy woman stole my beer. I shake my head and flag down the bartender for two more.

"This place is cute. I've never been here before," she chirps, taking another sip from the pilfered beverage.

Cute? It's a shithole. She leans back, her elbows resting against the bar. The neon light above her casts a soft blue glow across her face and makes those mischievous eyes of hers shimmer. My eyebrows knit together and I stare at her. She's happy. In a dive bar. Surrounded by drunks and degenerates. *Who is this woman?*

Her jaw drops and she starts bouncing when she sees the stage. "Is this a karaoke bar?" she asks.

I nod. "Open mic night." I point to the poster on the far wall, right above a table with a sign-up sheet.

She snaps her head to me and slides her slim fingers up my forearm. Her grip is firm but her hand is soft, delicate. Her short fingernails are painted a warm orange that pops against the dark ink of my sleeve tattoo.

"We *have* to sign up!" she says on an excited gasp.

"No." My muscles tense under her touch.

She glides her hand down my forearm before she pushes off the bar and turns to face me. "Yes."

I clench and unclench my fist, working the tension out. Raising my beer to my lips, I give her a quick once-over. "No."

She steps closer and my knees brush against her thighs. She grabs my shoulders and squeezes hard. "Yes," she declares.

I lift my hand from my thigh and navigate the small space between us, resisting the temptation to brush against her budding nipples. I slide my hand behind her neck and pull her to me. I lean forward to close the space between us.

Using a dead-serious tone, I grumble into her ear, "Not. Fuckin'. Happening."

I start leaning back, but she slides her hands from my shoulders to either side of my face and holds me right in front of her. She takes a minute, tilting her head to the side and examining me. I fight the urge to squirm away. She brushes a stray hair off my forehead and nods.

"Trust me, Big Man. This is *so* happening." She leans in and kisses me on the tip of my nose. Her smile is blindingly bright when she pulls away. She bounds off, shouting over her shoulder, "I'm signing up!"

I watch her swaying to the music and flipping through the songbook on the table. It's not until I go to sip my beer that I realize I'm smiling like a fucking idiot.

Surprise, surprise. Devin hasn't said much tonight. But it's not a brooding quiet. It's an attentive quiet. When a singer finishes, I lean into him and tell him what I think. He responds with one of his many grunts. He's taking in everything around him, but he doesn't feel the need to comment on all of it just to fill the empty space. It's refreshing.

He isn't bored or distracted. He's focused on me. He watches me sway my hips and sing along to the latest amateur singer up on stage. He isn't touching me, but I brush my body against his every few minutes to tease him.

The next guy takes the stage and we're in for a treat. He has to be over fifty if he's a day. He must have been going for silver fox, but, dressed in head-to-toe leather, he's ended up looking more like the poster child for a mid-life crisis.

He's rocking studded red boots, skin-tight low-rise leather pants and a cow-print jacket that may have been a rug in a previous life. I can't tell if the sheen on his bare chest is from sweating in all that leather or if he oiled himself up for the occasion. His long, stringy salt-and-pepper hair is pulled away from his face by a red silk scarf that matches those boots. He shakes his head, hops up and down a few times and points to the D.J. like the diva he is. Up on stage, he belts out an Aerosmith ballad at the top of his lungs.

He's the best of the night. Not because he can sing but for the sheer entertainment factor. The wannabe rockstar is in the zone, one hundred percent committed to his performance. I admire someone who throws themselves into something so completely. There is a heroism in his reckless abandon.

I peek over my shoulder at Devin. His face is stoic, as always. He cocks an eyebrow at me. I know that look. He uses that one on me often. That's his 'you can't be serious' look. He's mocking me. He's too cool to be enthusiastic about anything. *Ever*. But I know he's a faker, having fun even though I'd have to torture him to get him to admit it.

Wannabe finishes his solo with a flourish, dropping the mic, throwing his arms wide and dipping his head back. The place erupts in applause. I hoot and whistle in support. He hops off the stage with a simper and a wave, walking straight to me. He sidles up to the bar and I can't control my amused grin. Wannabe mistakes that as a sign of interest.

"You like my song, beautiful?" he asks, licking his wrist and applying salt in what I assume is a misconceived attempt at seduction.

"You were great. Very entertaining," I answer with a chuckle. He licks his salt, takes a shot of tequila and sucks on a lime while maintaining eye contact.

My eyebrow shoots up in Devin-like silent ridicule.

"It's all in the tongue." He licks his lips and leans in to me. I pull back.

The low growl from Devin behind me puts a smirk on my lips. Wannabe misreads the situation. He grabs my wrist. "How 'bout you ditch the statue and let me show you a good time?"

He just crossed the line from entertaining to creepy. I wrench my hand free and place it in the middle of his chest, pushing him away in an unmistakable rejection. *Yep, he's definitely oiled up.* I pull my hand away and gag at the slick mess covering it. Wannabe still doesn't take the hint and leans in again, dragging a finger along my exposed collarbone.

"Enough," Devin barks from behind me.

Tingles flood my stomach when he snakes his arm around my waist and pulls me against him. His body is cool, but the touch is searing. The connection burns through me. I lay my hand on top of his and close my eyes, focusing on his thick fingers spreading from the waist of my pants to just below my bra. His hold is firm and possessive. I've never wanted to belong to someone before, but I want to be Devin's now.

Wannabe is focused on Devin behind me and his lips twist into a pout.

I give him a little wink. "You know the best thing about statues? They stay rock hard all night. So I'm good. Thanks."

He chuckles, tips his shot glass to us and downs it before stalking off to find his next conquest.

Devin's grip tightens around me and I shiver, my body desperate to melt into his.

I twist in his arms just enough to meet his glare. I'm surprised at the real jealousy and a bit of annoyance in his features. I lift my hand to his face and stroke the scruff on his clenched jaw. "You almost lost me to a rock star there, Big Man."

His lips curl up at the edges in the closest I've ever seen to a smile. I nuzzle his nose and he responds with a soft hum. The rumble of the loud bar fades away as I stare into Devin's deep, dark eyes. More than anything, I want to break through that veneer he wears and hear the truth hiding in those soulful orbs. The arm locked around me makes him seem so strong, but his gaze is gentle. *Vulnerable.* I want to protect him.

I take the beer out of his hand and set it on the bar next to mine, twisting to face him full on. He's still sitting and I'm taller than him, tucked between his thick thighs. He glides his hands under my shirt, burning me with his icy touch. He massages my shoulder with one and slides the other to my lower back. Still cupping his face, I move a hand up under his shirt to rest on his bare pec. We're both fully dressed, but the skin-to-skin touch feels intimate. The people around us don't exist. We're in our own world. I am connected to him in a way I never want to lose. Dropping my forehead to his, I close my eyes and focus on the ragged breaths he takes and the heart beating under my palm.

I ease my lips to his, as if he'll break if I'm not careful. He tenses, but those lips stay soft, tender. He's on alert, but he's letting me in. He tilts his head and kisses me with such reverence, like he's confessing he's scared. He's begging me not to hurt him. My heart aches. I press my palm into his chest and deepen the kiss.

Chapter Eleven

Jessie

"Really? You like the pink one? But it's so girly," I tell Becs from the other side of the dressing room, my inner tomboy revolting.

She laughs. "I am a girl."

"No, you are a stunning young woman who needs to embrace colors outside the pastel family."

She laughs again, a light, easy sound. I wonder if that's what Devin's laugh sounds like. I'd love to hear it. *See him lighten up for half a second.* Despite what he seems to think, the world wouldn't crumble at the sight of Devin Bennett enjoying himself.

"Fine," she grumbles. "I'll try the green one." She reaches her arm out of the dressing room and I slap the green top into her outstretched fingers. "You're spending too much time with Devin. He's turning you into a control freak too."

A familiar tingle rushes across my body. *Devin hasn't rubbed off on me as much as I'd like him to.* No need to tell his sister that, though.

"I'm pushing you to become your best self, BB." I snicker. "Just like that sexy, grumbling big brother of yours."

She groans just like Devin. It's adorable. "I know he means well, but seriously, it's *my* life."

"Oh, I get it. I have *three* brothers."

Becs pops her head out of the dressing room. "*Three?*" she squeals.

I nod. "Jared, Jake and Jamie. Or the trio of terror, as I like to call them."

She ducks her head back in the dressing room. "Oh my God. Just one drives me crazy. How do you deal with three?"

"You get good at being sneaky. They don't need to know everything."

"What about your dad?" she asks, her words muffled as she either takes something off or puts something on.

"Oh, my dad is a pushover. My mom too. What about your parents?"

"Rob and Mandy are cool. They have rules and stuff, but they're not control freaks like Dev."

I twirl the strap of the dress I'm holding, debating how to ask what I want to know. "And your biological parents?"

"They're not in the picture at all," she answers without a twinge of emotion. "My mom ran off when I was only like six or seven and Dad ended up in prison on his third strike a couple years after that."

"I'm sorry. It's none of my business." I toss the dress to the side and stare up at the ceiling, kicking myself.

"It's not a big deal. Not for me, at least. Devin's always been there. He tried so hard to take care of me, but there's no way the state was going to give an eighteen-year-old full custody of a minor." The words roll off her tongue like she's answered all these questions before and it's old news. Still, my heart breaks for her a bit. I wish I was as strong as Becs Bennett.

"Rob and Mandy seem sweet."

"Oh, they're awesome. I love 'em." Her voice is tender, holding real emotion. "They can't have their own kids, so they let me get away with more than I should."

I laugh. "That sounds familiar. I'm the only girl, so my parents think I can do no wrong. I'm pretty sure they think I'm still a virgin."

Becs snort-laughs in the dressing room. Maybe talking to a seventeen-year-old about being sneaky and having sex isn't the smartest thing I've ever done.

I backpedal. "Not like there's anything wrong with being a virgin. I mean, sometimes I wish I'd waited until…" *When? When did you ever wish you'd waited?* I didn't think my little speech through and now I'm stalling, trying to think of anything else I could use to finish that sentence without being a total liar.

"Oh, that ship sailed last year." Becs fills in the silence. *Well, that answers that.*

"I'm going to take a wild guess—Devin doesn't know?"

She gasps and flings open the dressing room door. "Hell *no*! He'd kill Garrett if he ever found out."

She's exaggerating, but only a tiny bit. The kid who took Becs' virginity might not end up in the hospital, but Devin would break at least some of the smaller bones. A few fingers. Maybe an arm if the kid looked like a punk. My brothers threatened to do the same, especially Jared, the oldest and most pigheaded of the Allen clan. That's why I've made sure they never had positive confirmation of anyone I've slept with. Even the manliest of my ex-boyfriends knows to keep his mouth shut. It's like the sex witness protection program.

Becs steps in front of the full-length mirror, wearing the deep green top I picked out that matches her eyes. She smooths it over a bit, turning from side to side, the fabric swishing around her.

"Told you you'd look amazing."

She rolls her eyes, but there's a reluctant smile on her lips. "Okay, fine. You were right. I like it better than the pink."

"So, this Garrett. Is he your boyfriend?"

"No. Not anymore." A sadness settles in her eyes. Devin might not get a chance. I might kill this Garrett jerk myself.

I stand up, brush Becs' long hair off her shoulder and rub her back. "Do you want to talk about it?"

"Not really," she grits out, reminding me a bit too much of her brother. I decide to leave it alone, for now at least.

We finish shopping and I buy her the green top, and the pink one too because it's fun to spoil my pretend little sister. After, we meet up with Elizabeth for Mexican food. I'm nursing a margarita as we chow down on nachos and chat about life and boys and everything else. Not a bad afternoon, if I do say so myself.

"What's the plan for the next year, BB?" I ask Becs, taking a big bite out of a three-chip monstrosity piled high with all the toppings imaginable. Elizabeth and Becs stare at me like I'm disgusting. *Guess that's what growing up in a house full of boys will do.* "It counts as one nacho," I mumble through a mouth full of food, not helping my case.

Elizabeth slides a napkin across the table at me and averts her eyes.

"College, I guess," Becs answers with a noticeable pout.

"You aren't sure?" Elizabeth asks as I wipe sour cream off my forehead. *How'd it even get there?*

Becs lets out a defeated sigh. "I'm sure I'm going, I guess. Just don't know where."

"What's your top choice?" I ask.

Becs' eyes go wide, a spark lighting inside her. "Notre Dame. And I got in!"

"That's awesome," Elizabeth and I coo in unison.

The spark dies quick as lightning.

"Spit it out. What's the problem?" I nudge her on the bench seat next to me.

"My brother is the problem. Can you imagine how his head would explode if I told him I wanted to go to college across the country?"

"He loves you. If it makes you happy, I'm sure he'd be okay with it," Elizabeth says, ever the optimist.

"Have you met Devin?" I tease. "He likes change about as much as he'd like a public proctology exam."

We all laugh, but Becs' is half-hearted.

"First our mom took off, then his ex ghosted him right after high school. It's fair to say he's got a *thing* about the people he loves skipping town."

My ears perk up and my heart does laps in my chest. Becs already dropped the disappearing mom bombshell on me earlier, but now there's an ex-girlfriend too? "Ex?" I try—and fail—to sound casual.

"Yeah, Shawna. They were high school sweethearts. She left the day after they graduated. Tried to get him to go with her, but with our dad being a piece of shit and our mom being non-existent, that wasn't an option."

Jealousy burns deep in my veins. I hate Shawna. *How dare she try to get Devin to leave his family? His home? Tramp.* Holy crap, where did that come from?

Becs sips her horchata and pouts. "He stayed for me, so I guess I owe it to him to stay too."

The sadness in her young eyes breaks my heart. I grab her hand and squeeze it.

"Staying was his choice and I'm sure he doesn't regret it." *Good riddance, Shawna.* "And now leaving is *your* choice. He may be a grumpy jerk about it, but it's your life."

She squeezes my hand in turn. "Thanks."

There's an awkward silence, filled by the chomping of tortilla chips.

"You both graduate this year?" Becs asks after a few minutes.

"Yep," Elizabeth answers with a smile.

"Only a couple more months and I'll have a shiny new diploma with my name on it," I add.

"Then what?"

Elizabeth lights up like a freaking Christmas tree. "Med school at USF for me. Austin got into their social work master's program with a full scholarship." She beams while bragging about her boyfriend. It's too sweet for words.

"Grad school for me too. I'm getting my MBA."

"Where?" Elizabeth asks.

I shift in my seat. "Haven't quite decided that part yet." I've got a pile of acceptance letters in my drawer for schools across the country, but haven't picked one. It feels too final. As soon as I say yes, the rest of my life is set, stretching out in front of me in a boring, predictable, safe path.

Becs finishes chomping down on a chip and joins Elizabeth with the inquisition. "Then what?"

I pick salt off the rim of my glass. "I'm supposed to work for my dad. The family business. We own a handful of sporting goods stores my grandpa started forever ago." I take a long sip of my margarita, trying to hide the anxiety rising in the back of my throat.

"And you don't want to?" Elizabeth asks.

I heave a deep sigh. "No. Not really."

"Why not?" Becs quickly follows.

"Ever try and get excited about a jock strap?" We all laugh. "I love my family, but the idea of doing the same thing day in and day out? It sounds like torture."

"Then why are you gonna?" Becs asks. *This teenager is asking all the tough questions today.*

I let out a long sigh. "Because it's what I'm supposed to do. It's what my family wants."

"You're such a hypocrite!" Becs jabs from beside me.

"This is different, Becs." I sigh. "It's not like they're asking me to give up my dream college. I don't have some other great idea or burning desire. I just think spending the next thirty years knee deep in shin guards sounds...awful."

"Then do something else." Becs is relentless.

"It's not that simple."

"But it's *your* life." Becs uses my own words against me and I'm defenseless against her onslaught.

Elizabeth ping-pongs her stare between us, enthralled that I'm getting a lecture from a seventeen-year-old.

"Besides, you said your family was tight. I'm sure they'd understand."

"Understand or not, it'd still break my mom's heart."

"Isn't that a bit dramatic?" Elizabeth asks.

I shake my head. "You don't know my mom. My brother Jake was supposed to take over as the company's legal counsel after law school. Instead, he took a job with Legal Aid representing people who can't afford to hire an attorney. Fighting for the downtrodden and disadvantaged and all that. He's practically a saint, only more kickass. And you know what my mom said to him at Christmas last year?"

Elizabeth and Becs both shake their heads.

"She got this far-off look in her eye and said she was glad he could help *those* families. She knew she couldn't be mad at him because he was helping other people, but she was sad he didn't put *his* family first."

Becs blows out a quick breath. "Ouch. That's brutal."

"No shame compares to a mother's guilt trip." Elizabeth tries to joke, but her voice is a little too full of angst to pull it off.

"Right? And I'm supposed to live with that guilt every day until I die?" I shake my head and polish off my margarita. "I always thought I'd run off for a couple years after graduation and travel. Rebel a little and get it out of my system. But I don't know anymore."

"Something around here worth staying for?" Elizabeth teases. I toss my napkin in her face and tell her to shut up.

Becs has a grin a mile wide. "She's in love with my brother."

I gasp. "I am not."

"Are too," Elizabeth pipes up. *How did I end up getting double-teamed here?*

"We've only had one date."

"You guys can't keep your hands off each other," Becs teases in a singsong voice.

"Can too." My cheeks catch fire and I feel like a silly girl with a crush. That's what this is, just a massive crush.

"I fell in love with Austin the first week we were together. It just took me a little longer to realize it."

There is no *way* I could be in love with Devin. It's too soon. Sure, I'm crazy about him. The way his hands feel. The way he smells. Those dark eyes. The way he can say so much without saying a word. But that's not love.

Is it?

Chapter Twelve

Devin

I slam the last drawer to the rolling toolbox, cursing under my breath. "Mikey!" I holler across the bays.

"Yeah, boss?" he answers from behind me. I turn to see him wringing his hands.

"How many times have I told you to return tools after you're done with them?" I snarl. His eyes go wide. I take a deep breath instead of tearing into him like I want to. "Where the hell is the ten-millimeter socket?"

"Top drawer."

I shake my head. "That's where it's *supposed* to be. I asked where it *is*," I say through gritted teeth.

Mikey reaches behind me, pulling out the drawer I just finished searching. It takes all the self-control I have not to break his arm. He tries to slide it open, but I don't move. He can only crack it and squat down to peer inside.

"I swear it was in there this morning." He scratches his head in confusion.

"It's not now."

He swallows hard and scurries off with an, "I'll find it, boss."

I kick the toolbox behind me then curse myself for doing it. I'm not the destructive type. I keep my anger in check. I have to. But I've been on edge all week. This shop is a second home to me, but Jessie and her changes have me crawling out of my skin. I don't know where anything is. I don't know how to run my own damn shop. Sean and Shelley took to the system like ducks to water, but Mikey and I are fucking lost. And Jessie isn't even here to deal with it. She hasn't been here in days. Not since our date.

I haven't seen her since I dropped her off at her front door and got sent away with a chaste kiss. Her sugary-sweet smell is fading. Without her in my space, I'm adrift. I take a deep breath and hold it while I roll my neck. Memories of that brilliant smile and those hazel eyes torture me.

Fuck it.

I slam the office door behind me, drop into the chair and hit the Call button on my cell. I reach behind me and grip my neck as the ringing cuts through the silence in the small space. My heart is pounding in my chest. I hate talking on the phone. I hate *talking*, period.

"Devin?" Jessie's confused voice calls out to me.

"Yeah," I answer. The line goes silent. I pull the phone away from my ear to make sure the call is still connected. Yep, still ticking along. I hold the phone up to my ear again and hear Jessie's soft laugh. My chest gets tight and I run my fingers through my hair.

"I guess I should be flattered you called."

I groan.

"Oh no. That's your annoyed groan. What's up, Big Man?" Her words are labored and her breath is coming fast, like she's working out.

"Where are you?" I sound like a possessive douche.

"On campus. Missing me, aren't you?" The teasing lilt in her voice is obnoxious as fuck. I grunt. She giggles. "I miss you too," she adds. Her voice is playful, but soft and breathy, like she's whispering confessions to me. In bed. I close my eyes and focus on the sound.

The line goes silent again, but this time I know she's still there. There's a rustling then a long sigh.

"Well, then. It's been fun *not* talking to you—"

"I need you at the shop," I croak out.

"Need? I'm blushing."

If she was in front of me, I would kiss the hell out of that sassy mouth. I run my hand down my face to wipe off the stupid grin.

"Your system is a pain in my ass."

"Well, you shouldn't have shoved it up there," she deadpans.

I groan. She giggles. Our usual.

"I know I haven't been around the shop much. I've had to catch up on a lot here on campus. I've got a dodgeball game—"

"Dodgeball? How old are you?"

"Oh, hush. Not all of us were born a cranky old man." There's more rustling before she shouts, "I'm coming!"

She lets out a little sigh. "I've got a very *adult* game of dodgeball. Then I'll come see about that ass of yours. Alleviate the pain in those buns of steel. See you soon, Big Man."

She hangs up before I say anything. The itch that's been driving me crazy all week settles and I get back to finding that damn ten-millimeter socket.

A few hours later, Jessie bounces into the service bays like they're her own personal playground. She's wearing cut-off jean shorts and a loose white T-shirt. A long silver necklace draws my eyes down her chest, where I can just make out the bright pink bra barely containing those beautiful tits. Her sunshine-colored hair isn't up in its usual high ponytail. It's down and wild. The soft waves flow over her shoulders, held back by bright red-framed sunglasses perched on her head. She looks like spring, fresh and luscious. As usual, there is a wide smile on her lips and a mischievous glint in her eye. It takes all my willpower not to smile at her, too.

"Have no fear, people. Your digital savior is here," she sings through the space, and everyone stops what they're doing and turns to look.

She's like an eclipse, fascinating but deceptively dangerous. She makes me want to give in, to lose control — something I know from my family's violent history I can never afford to do.

I'm in the far bay, helping Mikey sort out a rats' nest of wires, one of which keeps causing an electrical short. His eyes are eating up Jessie's curves with a young hunger. He'd be a better fit for her, ready to have some fun and make the mistakes life hasn't taught him to avoid yet. I tap the pliers on the frame of the Toyota to catch his attention and point down at the problem at hand. He tears his eyes off Jessie and ducks back under the hood.

I glare at her while indulging in the sight of those long legs in those short shorts. She stops to give Sean a big hug, unconcerned with the grease and assorted shit on his overalls that's going to stain her white shirt. His hands stay on her sides, a friendly gesture, but it makes me curl my fingers into fists, eager to touch her. Sean leans down and says something in her ear. Her stare snaps to me and that dauntless persona drops for half a beat. When Sean pulls back, Jessie kisses him on the cheek. I let out a light grunt, jealous of the old hippie for the first fucking time in my life.

Jessie passes by Shelley's stall and gives her a fist bump. Shelley gestures to me over her shoulder. I can't hear what she says, but it's Shelley, so I'm *sure* it was X-rated. Jessie's eyebrows do that teasing wiggle, a soft pink covers her cheeks and she bites her lower lip.

After Shelley, mine is the only bay left. Jessie takes her time making her way over. She keeps her hazel eyes locked on me, that sexy grin on her lips. I stand tall, legs wide and arms crossed, watching her strut through my auto shop like it's a goddamn catwalk. She's the sexiest thing I've ever seen.

"Hot damn," Mikey murmurs next to me. He clears his throat and returns his gaze under the hood where it belongs. "Found our problem. Looks like the left turn signal." He thinks I can't tell he's been sneaking peeks at Jessie rather than doing his damn job. I don't bother acknowledging him. JB has my full attention.

She steps up to me, into me. She mocks my pose, legs wide and arms crossed. With a scowl that looks as natural as lipstick on a pig, she peers up at me, bats those long lashes and grunts. "Hey."

My control melts under the heat of my desire for this woman. I'm starved for her, and in this minute, I don't give a fuck who knows it. In a flash I cup her face and crash my lips on hers. She's surprised as hell, almost jumping out of her skin and letting out a startled yip. The sound makes me grin against her mouth. She recovers, breaking our kiss for the briefest moment before she unfolds her arms and wraps them around my waist, pulling me against her.

I'm vaguely aware of the shop going dead silent. We have an audience and I don't care. I tilt her head and deepen the kiss. She approves with a soft moan as her tongue dances with mine inside that sweet mouth of hers. I'm teetering on the edge, about to lose myself.

A wrench hits the concrete floor with an unmistakable clatter. Sean lets out a loud whistle and Shelley's voice echoes across the bay. "Get a room!"

Jessie pulls away and buries her face in my chest. Her body is shaking with a soft giggle. I slide one hand down her back and use the other to flip Shelley the bird. She harrumphs and returns to work. Sean too. Mikey picks up the wrench he dropped and wanders off to sulk on a smoke break.

Now that no one's watching, I lean down and bury my nose in Jessie's hair. I take a deep breath of that unforgettable vanilla smell and kiss the top of her head.

Jessie recovers her composure. "I hear you've got a pain in the ass."

I nod. "An annoying blonde one." I rake my fingers through her hair and fist a handful of it.

"You know you can't get enough of me." She shoves off my chest and struts back to the office. I watch every sway of her hips as I stalk after her.

She's right. I can't get enough.

Chapter Thirteen

Jessie

I make it to the office and take the few precious seconds of solitude I have to fan my face and take deep breaths. That body. Those eyes. *That kiss.* Sweet baby *Jesus*! He could kiss me all day, every day, until I die and that'd be just fine. His lips are like crack. I've been craving him all week. The taste of him. His manly mechanical smell. School has been crazy, all my study groups pulling extra hours with midterms looming, and my mandatory appearances at the sorority house and dodgeball on top of that. I've been working on pulling back, on saying no, but I still haven't had time to come see him since our date.

It's been torture. My fingers ache to dial his number. Or even the shop, just to hear his voice before I hang up. I'm trying to play a little hard to get. I've been chasing him so hard for so long that I need to step back and make sure he's in this too.

Our date was intense. Everything about Devin Bennett is intense. I'm good at fun. *Light. Easy.* This isn't that. This is the beginning of something. I feel it every time he touches me, and I need to know he wants me before I let this get out of hand.

I was ecstatic when Devin called me. Even if his side of the conversation consisted of more groans than actual words, my heart was racing the whole time. He was complaining about my system, but I'm hoping he was really complaining about not getting to see me more than anything else.

His heavy footsteps are quick behind me. I lock my playful expression in place.

"What seems to be the problem, Big Man?"

He shuts the door behind him and is on me in a heartbeat. He dips to hook his hands underneath my knees, lifting me onto the desk and pushing me back in one motion. He steps between my thighs and wraps his strong arms around me. His movements are purposeful—aggressive even, but his touch is feather soft.

He has one arm holding me to him while he explores me with the other. He traces along the racing pulse in my neck with rough, cool fingertips before dipping to tickle the exposed skin at my collarbone. I get lightheaded at the gentle caress, fisting a handful of his shirt to keep from flying away. I lift my chin and his lips take over from his fingers, worshiping me with languid kisses.

He slips his hand into my hair, massaging the nape of my neck. I hold his wrist, desperate to keep him, and arch my back, pressing into him. My mouth falls open. Ragged, shallow breaths are all I can manage.

He hasn't said more than a few words to me all week, but his actions speak so much. He missed me. I can feel it. And I'm not talking about the giant hard-on pressing into my thigh. It's the possessiveness in his touch. The obsession in his eyes. The pleading in his kisses. I feel it too. A need for him. It's consuming me.

He's leaning forward and my back is going to be pinned to the desk any minute now, at his mercy. He slides the hand at my back under my shirt and with a quick flick of his wrist, my bra pops open. *Damn, that's sexy.* I want him to take me. Right here. Right now.

Then what?

Then, I have no idea. If the tease is what keeps Devin coming back, I need to slow this *way* down.

"Whoa. Easy, Tiger." My voice is thicker than maple syrup.

Devin growls in my ear, but doesn't pull away. I push him away with my fist still balled around a handful of his shirt. He leans back, not fighting me. He locks his arm around me, holding us together. He grinds his hard length against the apex of my thighs, making me see stars. I want him, but I want there to be an *us* more.

I slide both my hands to his chest, smoothing out the wrinkled shirt. Again. I'm staring at his pecs, refusing to meet those coal-dark eyes that I'm sure are burning embers. I clear my throat, shaking the lust out of my voice before I try to reason with him.

"I'm not a sex-on-the-desk-before-the-second-date kind of girl." I'm trying to keep it light, despite the torture we're subjecting ourselves to. The truth is I *am* a sex-on-the-desk kind of girl. Let's get real. When it comes to Devin, I'm a sex-wherever-the-hell-we-end-up, dear-God-just-take-me-now kind of girl. But I'm aiming for girlfriend status here. And if he's *half* as good in bed—or on desk—as he is at kissing, I'll slip over the edge from pushy girlfriend into obsessed stalker.

I slam the brakes on our make-out session so fast it gives my vagina whiplash. *Sorry, girl.* Devin drops his head to my shoulder. He grinds his hips against mine again with a soft moan. Patience is a virtue Devin's thick cock does not possess.

"Second date. Tonight," he demands.

Desire clouds my mind, making it hard to find a coherent answer. "Can't," I answer on a pant. "Study group." I'm kicking myself for turning him down, but the guilt of bailing on my friends is too strong.

"Tomorrow," he demands in a deep, sexy rumble that makes my ovaries scream for more.

"Can't," I say again. Everything below my waist is begging me to reconsider. My heart is shaking in terror and my reason is barely holding on. "Family dinner."

He takes a deep inhale and nips at my neck, the frustration driving him crazy. "Friday?" he pleads.

I'm supposed to be at a frat party with Michelle on Friday night. I promised her I'd be there. Despite ditching me last time, she's still insisting she needs a wing woman. I fight against the guilt of flaking on her. We have a whole damn house full of sorority sisters dying to go to frat parties. *She can find someone else to be her wing woman for sure.* If I'm going to see Devin again any time soon, I need to say no to something else. I need to choose him.

"Okay. Friday."

One last grind and Devin breaks away from me and steps back across the room. He runs his hands through his thick black hair and glares at me. I bite my lip and press my legs together, missing the hardness of him against me. He is so dark. *Eyes. Hair. Soul.* He looks angry, but I know better. He is tortured and beautiful and I've never seen anything sexier.

Screw it. I slide off the desk, determined to get my afternoon delight. But before I can step closer, he's out of the door.

Chapter Fourteen

Jessie

Devin knocks on my door right on time for our second date. I get a flock of angry birds swirling around in my stomach when I see him standing on my porch. My mind slides back to the night we met. To that first kiss that ruined any other lips for me. I slide a hand up his chest and place a soft kiss on his cheek.

"Hi," I greet him.

He nods, cups my face and kisses me. It's not his usual soul-stealing variety. There isn't the usual desperation, like he's containing a wild beast inside him that will tear me apart. This is sweet. Familiar and intimate. It's how a groom kisses his bride after the 'I do'. It's chaste, but greedy. He kisses usually say 'mine'. This one says 'my darling'.

When he pulls away, there's a small smile on his beautiful lips. My heart skitters to a stop in my chest. Devin takes my hand in his and leads me to his car. The drive is quiet. I'm focused on sorting out my jumbled emotions and Devin, well, he's always quiet.

"Tell me about Shawna."

He takes me in with those dark eyes, his lips pursed and his eyebrows pinched together, making him look like an angry caveman.

"BB said she was your high school sweetheart."

He looks back out at the road and shakes his head. "Fuckin' Becs."

"So? Was she?"

He nods.

"What happened?"

"She left." His voice is hard. His grip on the steering wheel tightens.

"Why didn't you go with her?"

"Couldn't."

This is excruciating, but I'm going to drag the truth out of him, one one-word-answer at a time.

"Why not?" I scooch closer to him on the bench seat.

"Becs," he answers. That's not the whole answer, but I get it. *Family is family.*

"But you wanted to go?"

He doesn't answer. He slows as we pull into a parking lot and I know I don't have much time left before he makes an escape.

"Would you have left, with Shawna, if you could?"

He turns off the engine, gets out and slams the door. I let out a disappointed sigh and follow behind him. He waits at the front of the car for me and takes my hand again when I stand next to him.

He looks down at our interlocked fingers. "Maybe."

I nod. He raises his gaze up to me and there's so much hurt there. He's massive, strong and intimidating. But standing here, he's bare and vulnerable. I lean forward on tiptoes and kiss him. *My darling.*

Bowling. We're bowling. I have a feeling Devin is trying to keep things as casual as possible with these dates. He thinks he can chase me away with dive bars and bowling alleys. *Ha.* I have three brothers. Jake can burp the alphabet and Jamie thinks *pull my finger* is the height of comedy. I've got this. If he wants to chase me away, he needs to stop kissing me.

"These are sexy as hell," I deadpan, staring down at my ancient multicolor bowling shoes. "I don't know how you're going to be able to keep your hands off me."

He's sitting in one of the orange plastic chairs, tying his own sexy bowling shoes. I do a little spin in front of him and end it with a sexy model pose and a wink. He wraps his long fingers around my waist and pulls me to him while he stands. He's graceful for someone so big. Every motion of that powerful body seems thought out, planned. *Choreographed.*

"Maybe I don't," he mumbles, staring down at me.

"Balls," I say flatly. His eyes narrow in confusion. "We need balls." I skip off to find the perfect bowling ball. I settle on a neon lime-green eight-pounder. Devin has a monstrous black thing that weighs as much as I do. He lifts it like it's a box of Kleenex, the cords in his tattooed forearm flexing. *Damn.* Bowling isn't supposed to be a turn on, but when Devin struts down that alley and bends over to toss his ball, the muscles in his back rippling, I get hot and bothered. I squeeze my legs together and think of clipping my toenails and scrubbing my toilet.

Devin knocks down eight pins and picks up the next two on his second try. I'm not going to be winning this game and I couldn't care less. As long as I get to stare at Devin all night, I'll throw gutterballs until the end of time. He plops down across from me, spreading his legs wide and resting his arms on the back of the bench seating. He's got a damn smug look on his face. *Okay, Mr. Bennett. Let's play.*

I scoot around the ball dispenser thing and bend low in front of him, wiggling my butt in his face. He takes a deep breath and I peek over my shoulder, happy to see his eyes are locked on my ass. I'm definitely winning *this* game.

I grab my green ball and hurl it down the lane. It makes a beeline for the gutter, leaving all ten pins glued in place. *Not an ideal start.* I overcorrect on my second attempt and fling it down the other gutter.

"I need nachos and beer. That's the problem. Lack of sustenance."

Devin shakes his head at my declaration, but he nods when I stick out my thumb and pinky finger, holding them to my lips in the 'want a drink' gesture. He reaches for his wallet but I stop him with a glare. We lock eyes. He stalks over to me, shakes his head and slaps a twenty in my hand. *Guess he's buying this round then.*

The entire little argument about who's paying happens in a few seconds without us saying a thing. I like that I understand him without needing words. We could have an entire date without talking. I think Devin might prefer it.

Our game is almost over. Devin's managed three strikes, two spares and a handful of eights and nines. The best I've managed is a four and polishing off most of the nachos. It's the second to the last frame and Devin's got three times the points I do. The smug, lopsided smirk on his lips is unmistakable. I've never seen him happier than when he's beating me. I'm not worried. I've got this.

"I'm getting a strike on this roll. I can feel it," I declare. Devin quirks an eyebrow at me, taking a lazy sip of his beer. *Challenge accepted.* I pick up my lime-green ball and stage whisper, "Come on, Greenie. Let's show him what we've got."

I line myself up in the center of the alley. I keep my eyes locked on the head pin and focus on the smooth, fluid motion. My ball rolls down the lane, starting out straight and true. My heart ticks up. *Yes. Yes. Yes.* Then Greenie gets a little wobble. *No.* I lean to the right, trying to keep her on track. It doesn't work. Greenie keeps diving toward the gutter.

A stifled laugh, covered by a fake cough, sounds behind me. I spin and stare daggers at Devin, who's reclining in that ugly plastic chair like it's his blue-collar throne. Anger surges through my body.

"You know what a strike is, JB?" Devin asks when I flop into my chair. He picks up his ridiculous black ball and rolls it down the lane with impressive force. The pins go flying, parting like the damn Red Sea. He struts back to me. "That's a strike."

He winks. *Winks!* Who is this guy? He is playful and aggravating. I'm getting that damn strike if it kills me. I try to pick up his black ball, but the holes are too far apart. My fingers don't fit. I use both hands and scoop it up. Devin cocks his head at me, but I give him a hair toss and charge forward.

"Watch this," I tell him.

His voice is both sultry and condescending. "I'm watching."

Let's do this, Blackie. I take a deep breath and heave the heavy black ball with everything I have, hoping force will make up for aiming. Unfortunately, Blackie decides to go more up than forward. In a glorious arc, it soars forward before slamming down into the wood of the lane with a resounding thud that echoes across the alley. *Shit.* Can you get kicked out of a bowling alley? I'm about to find out.

I let out a loud gasp and slap my hands over my face. I spin back to Devin, eyes wide in panic. He's laughing. Not chuckling. Not giggling. *Laughing.* Out loud! It's a deep, rich exhilarating sound. I've been dreaming about this moment for weeks and every fantasy has fallen short of the majesty that is the sight of Devin Bennett laughing. His eyes are bright and light with crinkles in the corners. His luscious lips are curled up, revealing brilliant white teeth. Dimples aren't a cute enough word to describe the adorable dip that turns his strong jaw into a playground. He is irresistible. My heart melts, puddling in my hideous bowling shoes.

My arms fall limp at my sides and my mouth drops open. I stare at him in complete awe. His eyes go wide with concern and he points behind me. I turn to look, convinced the bowling alley bouncer is coming to toss me out on my ass. There's no burly bouncer. There's just Blackie, rolling down the alley, straight and true. The ball hits the first pin dead on and keeps going. It surges through all ten pins, each teetering over in submission. *Strike!* I got a strike. Hysterical, I jump up and down.

I run into Devin's arms, letting out a high-pitched victory squeal. He spins me around. I bury my face in the crook of his neck and let waves of pure happiness wash over me. Getting my first strike is nice, but it's nothing compared to being in his arms. It feels so damn good. Hearing him laugh, knowing he's let down that ton of bricks he carries around, even for just a second, is the best feeling in the world. He's happy.

I pull back and take in the gorgeous sight of his full, goofy smile. His teeth are white and straight, he's got small dimples popping — and those eyes. They're sparkling black pools of joy. My heart flutters in my chest. I feel so light I could take off like a rocket. *Where'd the gravity go?*

"I lo—" I slap my hand over my mouth and jump away from him like he's the electric chair and I'm the soon-to-be dead man.

How could I be that stupid? It was on the tip of my tongue. It almost slipped out! I'm not ready for 'I love you's. That's what couples say after months of dating. Serious dating, not sexually frustrated blackmail dating. It's a hop, skip and a jump to the world of 'marry me', 'I do', and 'it's a boy'! I'm not anywhere near there. I'm happy in Netflix-and-chill land.

Devin would look gorgeous in a tux, that wide smile on his lips, watching me walk down the aisle to him.

Gah!

What am I saying? That is insane. I *don't* want to get married. I'm not ready. This is all Elizabeth's fault. Her and Austin and their stupid sappy love story. That's great for them, but I'm not there yet. I'm barely ready for a steady boyfriend. My heart is thudding and my mind is racing dizzying laps.

Devin is staring at me, concern and confusion replacing that beautiful smile on his face. *Good.* That's safer. He takes a cautious step toward me.

"Shit. Sorry. I lost—" *My mind?* I bite my bottom lip and search the area around me for a believable lie. I rub my chest—it's a thousand degrees. "I lost...my necklace."

"Here?" Devin asks, his dark eyes falling to the floor. "What's it look like?"

Guilt rips through me as we both drop to our knees, searching for my imaginary necklace.

"Look like?" I ask, buying time. "It was just a thin gold chain."

Devin grunts in response, continuing to look. What is the appropriate time to let the man you're in love with search a dirty bowling alley floor for an imaginary necklace? Five minutes? Fifteen? Every second we spend scouring the tiny space is a knife to my stomach.

"Maybe I lost it at home, when I was changing."

"Want to go home and look?" Devin asks. I nod, needing some space to figure my shit out.

We're halfway to my house when he asks, "Was it special?"

"What?"

"The necklace."

Right. "No, nothing sentimental. Just thought it was pretty," I answer, hoping never to talk about the stupid thing again.

He walks me to my door, the tenderness of his large hand on the small of my back driving me crazy.

I crack the door and turn to him. "Thanks for tonight."

"You don't want me to help look?"

My breath catches at the thought of Devin in my room. Where my bed is. I've had my world rocked enough for one night.

"No, thanks. I've got it." I bite my lip.

"You okay?" He inspects me, rubbing my cheek with a rough thumb. My knees go weak.

"Yeah, I'm good." My voice is high-pitched and shaky.

Devin tilts his head and grunts. He knows I'm full of shit, but he's going to let me get away with it tonight.

"I had fun," he tells my lips. It's the mother of all confessions for Devin Bennett, Mr. Serious. I should be thrilled, but I'm too focused on keeping my mouth shut to respond.

I rest my hands on his thick waist when he steps into me, closing the small space between us. He brushes his full lips against mine, a tentative touch. A soft moan slips out. That's all the permission Devin needs to consume me. His kiss lights a path across every inch of my body. Warm, fuzzy tingles spread across my flushed skin and penetrate deep into my chest. His kiss is a claim on my body and plea to my heart.

He breaks the kiss, pulls back and watches me. His small smile restarts my heart. Without a word, he walks off into the night.

Yep. Definitely in love with Devin Bennett.
Shit.

Chapter Fifteen

Devin

I hand Austin a beer and sit on my couch next to him. He asked to come over for a 'serious talk'. Talking is as much fun as getting waterboarded to me, and Austin would rather get his balls waxed than be serious. The fucker would crack a joke at his own damn funeral. For him to ask to come over for a talk means some shit has got to be proper fucked. My guess is it's got something to do with Elizabeth. He lost his fucking mind when they broke up late last year, but they've been inseparable since he moved in with her a couple of months ago. How she puts up with his shit is beyond me. He crashed at my place for a couple of weeks and his dumb ass just about drove me fucking insane.

I tip my head back. "Well?"

Austin takes a long sip of his beer. He's sitting there, quieter than I've ever seen him. His knee is bouncing and he's picking the label off the bottle. I don't say anything, letting him take his time to spit out whatever the fuck is important enough to waste my Saturday night.

He shoots off the couch and paces like a caged tiger. I've never seen him so worked up. He's usually the king of calm, cool and collected. His smartass smirk is always locked in place. But not today. Today he's about thirty seconds from losing his shit. *It's glorious.*

"Just hear me out." He comes to a quick stop in front of the TV, wiping a hand down his exhausted face. He takes a deep breath and holds it, rolling his shoulders. "Okay, here it is."

I lean forward, bracing my elbows on my knees and giving him my undivided attention. His locks his eyes on me. He looks like he might throw up.

"I'm going to ask Elizabeth to marry me."

Fuck. I was not expecting that.

I'm careful with my words, knowing he's nervous as fuck. "You've only known her a couple months."

"I know. I know. But it seems like so much longer than that."

"It's not."

Austin sighs. "I didn't come here to argue about calendars and bullshit."

"What did you come here for?"

"To figure out if I'm fucking insane."

"You're insane," I deadpan.

"Fuck you."

He sits on the couch. We drink our beers in silence.

"I love her, man. So much." Austin's voice is soft and sincere.

"Why do you want to marry her?"

"Because I love her?"

"Marrying her gonna change that?"

Austin pauses, thinking. "No."

"Then why do you want to *marry* her?"

I'm no expert on relationships, but I know it doesn't matter how much two people love each other if they don't want the same thing. They'll walk separate paths. I shake my head to get rid of Jessie's beautiful, haunting smile.

"Marriage is serious. You can't take that shit back."

"I know." Austin's voice has a defensive bite. He takes a long pull of his beer.

"So why?" I ask again, watching him from the corner of my eye.

He takes a deep breath in through his nose and looks up at the ceiling. "She's the one, man. She's beautiful. Smart. Sweet. Sassy. Loving. Sexy as fuck without even knowing it. She's everything." He sits up and stares into the distance. I swear I can see the lightbulb switch on. "And I want to be with her for the rest of my life. Wherever she's going, I'm going. She's home."

I turn to look at him full on, seeing the truth in his words. I hold out my beer. He clinks it in a toast.

"Congrats." I stand and we share a quick hug with plenty of back slaps.

"Thanks."

He's still brimming with energy, but now it's more excitement than anxiety. I couldn't be happier for him, but a cold ache tightens in my chest. What he has is rare. Something I might never find.

"Holy shit, I'm getting married!" Austin says on a satisfied sigh.

"She has to say yes first."

"Fuck off. Who could say no to this?" The idiot points up to his cheesy-ass grin and I shake my head at his giant ego. "Speaking of making the ladies scream yes, how's it going with Jessie?"

"Like cuddling up with a hand grenade. One more shitty date and she'll be out of my hair."

"Shitty?" Austin asks.

I nod. "She promised to leave me and my shop alone if she got three dates. I'm making sure it ends at three."

Austin chuckles. "And how's that going for you?"

"She thinks everything is fucking sunshine and rainbows. That woman could find something good to say about a goddamn apocalypse." I let out a deep sigh and take a long pull of my beer.

"Exhausting, isn't it?" Austin goes doe-eyed, thinking about Elizabeth again, no doubt. "But it's kind of amazing too. Like seeing the world through the eyes of a kid. Everything is new and exciting."

I grunt a lukewarm agreement and nod. Jessie's insistence on being excited about the most mundane shit is obnoxious, considering I'm trying to get rid of her. But Austin's right. There's something endearing about it at the same time. Her optimism is contagious.

"Why does it have to end at three? Elizabeth thinks you two'd be great together."

I narrow my eyes at him, grumbling at his stupid-ass idea. "Your girlfriend doesn't know shit about me."

"Doesn't mean she's wrong." Austin sips his beer and smiles.

"Yes. It does." I'm not going to deny there's a fire raging between Jessie and me, but it will burn out quick enough. Girls like her don't stay with guys like me. They marry bankers or CEOs, not tattooed mechanics. I'm nothing more to her than a way to pass the time.

Austin shakes his head at me. Falling in love has rotted his brain. "I'm just saying, why rush it? Have fun and see where it goes."

"I know where it's going."

"No. You know where you're gonna *keep* it from going."

I shake my head. "I'm too old for college girls and their bullshit."

"Dude, you're twenty-five, not fifty."

"I know what I want. Where I'm going. Don't need to waste a couple years on someone still trying to figure it out."

Austin rolls his eyes, something he's picked up from Elizabeth. "You're not going anywhere."

"Exactly."

"That wasn't a compliment."

"Says you." I take the last sip of my beer and make my way to the kitchen.

"Come on. I know you're into her." Austin stalks into the kitchen behind me, tossing his beer into the trash. I glare at him as I pull the bottle out of the trash and toss it into the recycling under the sink.

"Sorry, gramps," Austin quips, holding his hands up in surrender. I pop the tops on two new beers. "What do you have to lose by giving this thing with Jessie a shot?"

"You lose your balls when you turned into cupid or you just tuck them up your ass so they fit in that diaper?"

Austin keels over with a laugh. I stalk over to the living room. Sinking into the couch, I flip on the TV and try to ignore my dumbass best friend.

"Fine. I'll leave it alone," he claims from behind me. "But don't come crying to me when she's got someone new chasing after her."

I groan and turn up the TV.

Chapter Sixteen

Devin

I slide my key into the lock of the shop door early as fuck Tuesday morning, only to realize it's already been unlocked. My shoulders tense and my senses are on alert. I know this door was locked last night because I was the one who locked it. *Something's not right.*

I ease into the shop, set my gym bag on the seat and step in without making a sound. I search the space, looking for signs of damage or something missing. Nothing seems out of place. Soft voices draw my attention to the back office. I notice for the first time that the light is on. Someone is here.

I ball my fists up at my sides and stalk over. The door is cracked, so I peek in, trying to get an idea of what I'm stumbling into. My pulse skyrockets when I see Jessie's beautiful smile and bright eyes. She's leaning close to someone and nods in silent encouragement. I drink in the sight of her, from her bright green toenails to her sunshine yellow hair. My mouth curls into a snarl at the sound of a man's voice.

Kicking the door open, I glare at Jessie and her early morning companion. They both jump, startled at the interruption of their private meeting. Jessie's breath catches in her throat and she slams a hand across her heart, that I hope is racing as fast as mine. I turn my accusing gaze to the man. *Mikey?* What the fuck is Mikey doing here? At the ass crack of dawn? With Jessie?

I narrow my eyes at him and wait for an explanation. He raises his hands and opens his mouth.

"Jesus! You scared the crap out of me," Jessie pipes up before Mikey can.

I cross my arms and take her in with a glare. She crosses hers to match, her eyebrow rising along with the side of her beautiful lips in a lopsided grin. She's fucking teasing me. *Taunting me.*

The three of us stand there in the early morning silence, Jessie and I warring in stillness and Mikey caught in the crossfire.

"I'm going to grab some donuts before we open." Mikey stands and shuffles to the door. I grunt in response and step into the small office so he can get by. He stops in the doorway and smiles at Jessie. "Thanks, Jessie." Mikey looks over at me, but refuses to meet my eyes. I don't want to believe there is anything going on between them, but there's a shameful blush on the kid's face that confuses the shit out of me.

"Any time, Mikey," Jessie coos back.

He closes the door behind him, sealing me and Jessie into the tiny office as if we weren't already locked in this standoff.

"What was that?" I ask.

Her smirk widens to a full grin. "That? Was none of your business."

"This is *literally* my business," I countered.

She sighs. "I was just giving him some pointers on the new system."

"At six o'clock in the morning?"

"I'm not a clock, Big Man. You want to know the time, get a watch."

She tries to brush past me, but I step in front of the door, blocking her escape. I'm peering down at her, still waiting for my straight answer.

She slides both her hands under my shirt, tracing her hot palms up my chest. A low moan escapes my lips as she presses a soft kiss on my chest, over my shirt. I can't remember my name, much less what the fuck it was I am supposed to be getting out of her. All I'm interested in is feeling more of her body pressed against me.

"I missed you," she whispers and my heart soars.

I wrap my arms around her and kiss the top of her head, lingering while I inhale her intoxicating scent. She relaxes into me, resting her cheek against my chest.

"I was helping him with the new computer system," she confesses.

"What'd he have to do to get a private lesson?" I ask, gravel in my voice.

She pulls away, peering up at me with those soft hazel eyes. "Ask."

"That all?" I mumble, brushing my nose against hers and inching my way to her lips.

She hums against me.

"Teach me, JB." I suck her bottom lip into my mouth.

"Say please." Her sultry voice is honey in my ears as I deepen our kiss, sliding my tongue into her warm, wet mouth.

I pull back and look down at her. She's a puddle of mush, a sappy grin on those kissable lips. I release her with a quick chuckle, walking away to prove to myself I still can.

"I've got work to do." I stride to the desk and aimlessly shuffle some of the paperwork sitting there, distracting myself from the tightness in my pants—and my chest.

"You're such a tease." She fans herself and flops against the door.

"Look who's talking."

"Tell me, Big man. When and where is date number three?" She bites her bottom lip, the one I was just sucking on. It's red and swollen from my handiwork.

"Tonight?" That was supposed to be a statement.

"Can't." She blows out a sigh like she's disappointed, but I can't help but feel like she's playing games with me.

I ball my hands into fists and lean against the desk on my knuckles. "Hot date?" I ask, not hiding my frustration.

"Kind of." She shrugs and watches me. We're staring at each other from across the room. I refuse to ask, but I'm desperate to know who she's planning on spending the night with instead of me. "My sorority is throwing our annual party. Tonight promises to be an epic debacle full of drunken debauchery."

"It's Tuesday."

"All day. Now that we've established both the day and the time, how about you pick another day?"

"Skip the party."

"I can't."

"You can."

She shakes her head and sighs. "I wish. I really can't."

I shake my head, not believing her. I push off my desk and go back to shuffling papers around without a purpose, refusing to look up at her when she shoves off the door and walks around the desk. She gives me a hip check before hopping up on the desk next to me. My fingers itch to wrap around her bare thigh brushing against me.

"I swear. I would ditch if I could." I let out a half-groan, half-laugh at her bullshit. "I have to be there. I don't know if you've met many sorority girls, but they need adult supervision. I'd ask you to come, but we both know you'd hate it."

She grabs the collar of my shirt and pulls me between her open legs.

"Come here, you grump-o-saurus rex." She tugs me down and I let her. She drops her forehead to mine and stares into my eyes like she's trying to communicate telepathically. I wish I could read her mind.

"If you're too busy, forget about it," I bite out, sick of being played with.

"Forget about what? Our third date?" She gasps. Climbing me like a fucking jungle gym, she wraps her legs around my waist and her arms around my neck. It's more playful than sexual. "Nice try. But no. How many times do I have to tell you, Big Man? This is happening."

Chapter Seventeen

Devin

Jessie has yet to balk at anything I've thrown at her. Nothing has managed to chase the determined pixie away. I'm getting desperate. The quicker I get her out of my life, the better. This is date number three and I'm counting on it to put the final nail in the coffin of Jessie's infatuation with the idea of us. Barbie and the bad boy. *Not going to happen.* I'm not going to let myself get wrapped up in something I know has no future.

I side-eye her sitting across the car from me. Her mask of perpetual cheerfulness slips as I pull up to the empty, dark strip mall. The solitary lamp post in the middle of the parking lot manages to highlight the shadiness of this joint. Half the stores are closed, shuttered up with graffiti-covered plywood. The other half advertise payday loans and massages with happy endings. This is my old neighborhood, where I grew up. *Dirty. Seedy. Tattered. Abandoned.*

"Are we getting matching tattoos?" She leans towards me on the bench seat, teasing me with those ruby lips.

I lick my lips, picturing marking her virgin skin. My name scrawled across her thighs. My initials carved into her heart. The idea of branding her, claiming her, is tempting.

I bite the inside of my mouth and turn my head to hide the smile. The damn thing keeps popping up around her. It's not the only thing *popping* up either. One whiff of her unique scent or a glimpse of those tan curves and I'm desperate to touch her. It's a compulsion.

I shake my head. "Not unless you want hepatitis."

She crinkles her nose. "Hard pass."

I climb out of the car and circle around to the trunk. Her soft footsteps follow me. I hand Jessie two putters and two golf balls. She lights up at the familiar mini-golf paraphernalia. When I pull out the flashlight and bolt cutters, she recoils with a stifled gulp. I let out a dark chuckle. *This is going to be fun.*

I grab her hand and pull her down a small alley between two buildings. I make a show of it, looking around and hunching forward as I slide the bolt cutters onto the fresh padlock. She's staring at the twisting metal, eyes wide.

"Keep a lookout," I whisper hiss at her.

She whips around, with a gasp. "Shit. Sorry."

She's bouncing with nervous energy, but she's going with it. I'm impressed. I thought she'd stop us long before we'd gotten this far. Demand I take her to get froyo instead of some light B&E. I've done this a few dozen times. It's a rite of passage around here, but she doesn't know that.

After a few minutes of failing with the bolt cutters, I kneel and take a look at the new lock. It's hardened steel. *Guess the owner got sick of buying new ones.*

"Well, fuck." I shake my head. *Froyo it is.*

Jessie peeks at me over her shoulder. "Just cut the chain." Her voice is light and playful.

I look at her in amazement. "You a little hellraiser, Jessie Bird?"

"Bet your sweet ass, Big Man," she says with a wink. Fuck, this woman might just be perfect.

I slice through the cheap chain like butter and pull open the door, ushering Jessie into the darkness. I slide in next to her, letting the door close behind us, shutting out the sliver of light from the alleyway. Dropping the chain and the bolt cutters with a metallic clatter, I wrap an arm around her waist and pull her into me.

"Having fun yet?" I ask in the pitch black.

She spins in my grasp, pulling me down to her while she stands on her tiptoes. "You always keep me on my toes, Devin Bennett." She brushes her lips against mine and my tongue dips out of its own accord to taste her. She slaps my chest and giggles. The sound shoots acid into my veins, burning across my body.

"What is this place?" she asks.

I slide my hands to her hips and turn her around. I flick on the flashlight and hand it to her. The small beam of light cuts through the darkness. Jessie takes a tentative step forward, spotlighting the Eiffel Tower, the Statue of Liberty, the Pyramids, Mount Rushmore and the Leaning Tower of Pisa.

She spins and I squint when I get a face full of flashlight before I can put my hand up.

"Mini-golf?" she squeals. Is there anything this woman won't get excited about? Her enthusiasm is fucking exhausting.

I shake my head and the flashlight drops. I can't see her, but I know the wheels are turning in her head. I can just make out when she holds up the putters in accusation.

"Mini-golf is boring. This is strip putt-putt."

"*Strip* putt-putt?" she asks. I grunt in affirmation. "You're going down, Bennett."

"That's on the agenda too," I growl, reaching out for her in the darkness.

She slips of out of my grasp, graceful as a dancer.

"Not so fast. Let's see what kind of moves you've got first." She struts off to the first hole, my flashlight and gaze following the sway of her hips the whole time.

I drop my ball, grip the flashlight between my teeth and line my shot up underneath Lady Liberty's skirt.

"Wait!" Jessie screeches right before I take my swing.

I grumble. Her flashlight rushes up and down my body.

"You've got more clothes on. It's not fair."

"We're even."

She ticks off every item of her clothing on her fingers. "Bra, panties, two shoes, shorts and shirt. Six." Hearing her say the word *panties* brings the image of her flashing me that tight ass in the office, and I release my lecherous smile.

"Six. Same," I tell her.

She scoffs, counting my clothes off on her fingers. "Two boots. Two socks. Boxers, pants, and shirt. Seven."

I lock my hooded eyes on her and give her a devilish grin. "No boxers."

Her throat bobs. "Briefs?"

I shake my head.

"Banana hammock?"

A laugh barrels out of my chest with such force that I keel forward and have to brace my hands on my knees to keep from toppling over. Her light laugh mingles with mine, filling the deserted shop around us.

She trains her flashlight on my junk with purpose. "I'm not sure how to process the fact that the only thing between me and *little* Big Man is a thin pair of jeans held together by a single flimsy zipper." She fans herself and lets out a ragged breath. "Take your shot before my ovaries explode."

I adjust my aim for the warping of the ancient, musty Astroturf that's impossible to see in this light. It's a hole in one. Jessie gives me a mocking golf clap.

"Should I just hand over my panties now?" she quips.

I moan in approval, holding out my hand.

"Down, boy. Don't let the perkiness fool you. I'm a fierce competitor."

She takes a shot, the Astroturf sending her ball spiraling into the dark abyss.

"Well, shit." She hands over her right flip-flop, and I've never enjoyed a game of mini-golf so much in my life.

Four holes in and she's down to her bra and panties. My hands are sweating as I choke up on my putter. I take a long, slow breath in through my nose and hold it while I swing. I shank it, my ball bouncing off Teddy Roosevelt's chin and back at me. Jessie lets out a long breath. I'm not sure which one of us is more nervous…or more disappointed I missed.

"My chance at redemption. Out of the way, Big Man." She wiggles in front of me, the thin fabric of her soft pink panties brushing against my groin and driving me crazy.

She nails it, sinking her first hole in one of the night. She jumps up and down, barefoot and beautiful. "Yes. Yes. YES!" she shouts, her full tits bouncing in the soft glow of our flashlights.

I'm a fucking paragon of restraint for not taking her against the stupid fiberglass Mount Rushmore.

She points a finger at me. "Shirt. Off. Now."

For once, I'm happy to do as she asks. I tug up the hem of my shirt, luxuriating in the hunger lingering in her eyes.

"Wait." Her breathy voice calls out. I let my shirt drop and stare at her. She crooks a finger with a naughty glint in her eyes.

I close the space between us. She bends down, positioning her flashlight so that it's shining up at us. For the first time, I get a good look at her lacy bra. Her nipples are peeking through the thin fabric and more than anything I want to suck one into my mouth. But I stand stock-still, waiting for her to make a move.

She dips her fingers inside my shirt, her slow strokes an excruciating tease tickling the skin above my jeans. I flex my abs and let out a rough moan at the contact. She gathers the cotton material, lifting it up and over my head. She tosses the shirt on the floor, discarded like the rest of her clothes and inhibitions. She adds her wet lips to the fingers caressing my chest. She flicks my nipple with her tongue, just about bringing me to my knees.

Digging my fingers into the soft flesh at her sides, I tug her to me. I grind into her, letting her feel not-so-little Big Man, in all his full-mast glory. She slides her arms around my neck and pulls me down to her. Her mouth is demanding, devouring me in the dark. She curls her fingers in my hair, tugging as she moans into my mouth.

We go from zero to a hundred in half a heartbeat. I slide my hand down her back. Finding my way inside her panties, I grab a handful of her perfect ass. She moans in approval and hooks her leg around my hip.

I glide my fingers further into her panties to find her soaking wet. The sound that leaves my throat when I feel her wet pussy on my fingers is primal and possessive. *Mine.* I unlock my lips from hers and latch on to her neck, desperate to mark her. I nip and suck at the soft flesh as I slide a finger inside her.

"Devin." Her sweet voice calling my name slices me open.

She tosses her bra aside and I suck her hard nipple into my mouth like I've been dreaming about doing all night. I back her against the Eiffel Tower.

She clings to me, her breath shallow and desperate in my ear. I slide my hand between us for a better angle and plunge two fingers into her tight pussy. She feels so fucking good. *Too good.*

I graze her clit with my palm while I pump my fingers into her. She digs her fingernails into my shoulders and I know she's leaving her mark on me.

"Devin. Yes. *Yes.*" My name on her lips, she comes apart in my arms and I'm a goner. This woman will be my undoing.

I claim her mouth again, swallowing her moans. I'm still gliding my fingers in and out of her, milking every

Amelia Kingston

ounce of pleasure from her gorgeous body, when she tugs open the buttons on my jeans. I want to be inside Jessica Allen more than I want my next breath.

"Hey!" A man's voice echoes through the dark room. "This is private property."

Goddamnit.

Jessie freezes like a deer in headlights, her hands still on my fly. I kick the flashlight away and cover her with my body to make sure no one gets a peek at what's mine. Jessie starts shaking. She's terrified.

"It's all right," I tell her, cupping her face and giving her a soft, reassuring kiss. Her shaking stops, but I still don't think she's breathing.

"You can't be in here." The stern voice is getting closer and the flashlight zeroing in on us from the other side of the Eiffel Tower.

"Hold up, Bobby," I call, my voice hard as rock.

"Dev?" The voice softens. "That you, man?"

"Yeah. It's me. And I need you to stop where you are and give me a minute."

Bobby's flashlight snaps to the front door and he lets out a light chuckle. "I got you, man."

When I pull away from Jessie, her face is bright red and she buries it in her hands. I grab my shirt off the floor and hand it to her to cover herself up while I go in search of the rest of her clothes scattered across the past few holes.

Standing shirtless in the empty parking lot, staring at Bobby's stupid grin, isn't how I saw this night going. He's nodding, eyes wide in anticipation, waiting for me to give him some juicy details. I ain't telling this clown shit. He shakes his head and chuckles.

"Should've given me a heads up, dude. I wouldn't've cock-blocked if I'd known..." Bobby's words trail off when Jessie steps out into the parking lot, fully dressed again and not able to look at us.

"Don't worry about it." I sock him in the shoulder for staring just a little too long at Jessie.

Jessie hands me my shirt. I slip it on and try to ignore the fact that it smells like her. I hope she smells like me too. Even in the dark there's a blush burning across her face. I feel like shit for putting her in this position. I meant to push her limits, push her away, not embarrass her to death.

"I'm Jessie." She holds out her hand to Bobby, who gives it a vigorous shake.

"Bobby." He's grinning like the fucking Cheshire Cat, looking between Jessie and me.

"Nice to meet you."

An awkward silence surrounds the three of us. *Take the fucking hint, dude.*

Bobby leans closer to me and whispers, "Nice."

"Jesus fucking Christ," I grind out. My friends are fucking idiots.

Jessie's eyes snap closed and she lets out a loud, self-conscious laugh. I grab her hand and tug her toward the car.

"Your putters," Bobby calls to my back.

"Keep 'em," I growl, opening the passenger's-side door for Jessie, and she slides in.

"Nice to meet you too, Jessie." Bobby gives her a stupid finger wave. She holds up a hand, pink surging on her cheeks. I slam the door and shoot Bobby a death stare.

Jessie is creepy quiet the whole way to her place. She's never quiet. I feel like shit. I fucked up, but I'm not good at apologies. I glance over at her. She's watching the world pass by, an empty look on her face.

I clear my throat. "Bobby's an asshole."

"He's not the only one." Her voice is soft, but her words are brutal.

"Excuse me?" I grit out.

"You heard me." She doesn't waver, her tone easy and aloof. She's fucking pissed.

She turns to face me, eyes boring into the side of my face for asking a fucking stupid question. I keep my gaze locked out through the windshield, trying not to squirm under her angry glare. Silence engulfs us. I love silence. Quiet is my peace, but this isn't that. This is torture. I'm used to her constant chattering. Teasing or seducing—she's always talking. Except now. Now I'm not worth her words and it's a knife to my fucking gut.

She's opening her door and jumping out before I've even come to a complete stop in front of her house. I turn off the engine and chase after her ass. By the time I make it to her, she's got her keys in the door. Something tells me that if she makes it across that threshold, I'm not going to see her again. A few hours ago, that was the goal. I was trying to chase her way. *Mission accomplished. Let's throw a fucking party.* Now I care enough to fight with her.

I wrap an arm around her waist and brace against the doorframe to keep her from pulling us forward. *From pulling away.*

"Sorry. I fucked up. I didn't think we'd get caught," I say into her soft hair.

She crosses her arms. Her back is straight and her body is tense. I squeeze her tight, silently asking for a response.

"Oh, so you don't usually get caught with your putt-putt hook-ups?" Her words are fierce, but her voice sounds shattered.

"Usually?" I ask her.

She spins, snakes her arms between us and shoves me back. She's slippery and strong like a damn ninja.

"Yes. *Usually*. As in all the other hundreds of girls you've taken to your secret playground. Your shady den of sex."

I laugh. I can't help it. She pins me to the sidewalk with a look that could kill me dead. I'm quick to wipe the smirk off my face. She's not pissed we got caught. She's jealous. I fucking love that she's jealous.

I hold up my hands. "I haven't taken anyone there since high school. It's closer to a den of teenage dumbfuckery."

Jessie's stare softens, meaning she's picturing punching me in the dick instead of full-on castration. I take a slow step towards her.

"You're saying that's not your go-to take-down spot?" She asks. "Show a girl the world and she'll show you a good time?"

I shake my head, not fighting the stupid grin spreading across my face. "Just you."

She reaches out and grabs the collar of my shirt. "Keep it that way."

"Yes, ma'am." I ease into her, inching my lips to her. She doesn't pull away.

"I'm not going to be some girl you can fuck and forget."

"No, you're not."

Her voice is shaky when she confesses, "This is important to me. You..." Her eyes go soft and she swallows hard before continuing. "Are important to me."

I cup her face, snake my fingers into her hair and kiss the everloving shit out of her. I leave no doubt that she's the only woman I've been thinking about. The only one I can't get out of my head. Or my heart.

Chapter Eighteen

Jessie

I'm doodling on my notebook while Trevor drones on about something. I started this study group Freshman year. I don't need it, but I'm the glue that keeps it going. If I'd stopped texting everyone and bringing in new members, it would have died off after that first semester. But tonight I couldn't care less. All I can think about is how my three dates with Devin are over. I promised him I'd leave him alone now. Stay away from the shop. I'm not sure that is a promise I'm able to keep.

Someone calling my name pulls me out of my haze.

"Sorry, what was that?" I ask.

"Did you have the notes from last Wednesday?" Andrea, the newest member of our group, asks.

I make trumpet noises and pull my notebook out of my backpack with a flourish. "Jessie's unparalleled note-taking skills to the rescue."

"Awesome! I'll go make a quick copy for everyone." She prances off and I'm jealous, missing the days I was that carefree.

Trevor takes the empty seat next to me. "You okay? I haven't seen you in forever. And you seem kind of out of it."

"Yeah. Fine." I slap my notebook closed, hiding my doodles. "Just have a lot going on lately."

"Are you sure? You always have a lot going on."

"Marvelous, darling. Simply marvelous," I drawl.

"Tiptop?" he asks with a boyish lopsided grin.

"Shipshape."

"A-okay?"

"Yep." I break routine with our standard playful banter. We usually go five or six rounds with cutesy salutations, but I just don't have the patience tonight.

"Well..." He runs his hands through his hair and blushes. "We could go grab a bite? If you wanted to talk or anything."

I've known Trevor since the second day of our Freshman year. And I've known he's had a crush on me since the third. We flirt and tease—I even let him kiss me on New Year's once—but he's never been anything serious. He's one of a million distractions that doesn't seem so fun anymore.

"I'm actually seeing someone." It might be an exaggeration, but it doesn't feel like a lie.

"Oh, wow." His eyes go wide and his jaw drops open. "Since when?"

"A few weeks now." I smile, remembering the past few weeks with Devin. The first time he touched me. The first time he kissed me. The first time he growled at me. I'm not ready for our firsts to be over.

"Congrats, I guess," Trevor adds with a dejected lilt. *Poor guy.* He never had a chance, but I guess he doesn't know that.

"Thanks. It's been hard finding time to see him, but we're trying." I swallow hard and press my lips together tight. I might as well just tell him. "In fact, I think I'm going to stop coming to study group. For a little while at least."

"Oh," Trever says, crestfallen.

"I'm sorry. I've just got so much going on and I just don't have the time anymore." Guilt dumps over me like a bucket of ice water.

"But you're still going to be on the volleyball team next month, right?" he asks.

I wince and shake my head. "I told Maddy I'm not going to be able to play."

He's nodding but frowning. I feel like I've kicked a puppy. I want to take it back, tell him I'll be there, but I won't let myself. I picture Devin's dark eyes to keep myself focused on what I really want.

"I...I'm sorry," I stutter.

"Don't worry about it. The year's almost over anyway. Had to end sometime, right?"

And with that, it's over. I said no and the world didn't end.

My phone buzzes in my pocket and I'm thankful for the excuse to cut off the awkward chat. "Sorry, it's my mom. Gotta take this."

He nods and turns his attention to Andrea.

"Hey, Mom."

"Jessie Bird! It's so lovely to hear your voice. It will be even nicer to see your beautiful face this weekend."

Crap. I forgot it's family dinner this week. "Yep. Looking forward to it."

"Are you bringing that new boy?"

"Boy?" I laugh. Devin is many things, but I think he stopped being a 'boy' about a decade ago.

"Jake said you've been seeing someone…"

I blow out a deep breath. *My middle brother has a fat mouth!*

"Oh, that. It's pretty new," I deflect.

"Is it serious?" Mom presses.

The line goes quiet. I can't lie to her, but I sure as hell can't tell her I'm in love for the first time in my life, either. She'll be picking out wedding dresses and baby names in five seconds flat. Mom's been dreaming about my wedding since the day I was born.

"It's…um…" *Shit.* "We've only had three dates."

"Jessica Bridget Allen, that isn't an answer."

I sigh. "Yes. It's serious. On my side at least."

She lets out a giddy squeal that an almost sixty-year-old woman has no business making.

"Calm down, Mom. It's still new."

"My Jessie Bird has a serious boyfriend! I thought this day would never come."

"What does that mean?"

"Oh, nothing, darling. You and Jamie are just like your father. All flirt and no falling in love."

"Huh?" That's the first time I've ever heard my dad called a flirt. He's never even looked at another woman.

"He swore he'd never get married. But when he fell, he fell hard." Her voice is wistful and sappy. "So, you're bringing him."

It's not a question. It's a command.

"I'll ask. I don't know what he's got going on this weekend."

"Pish posh. Tell him I'm making pot roast. He'll come."

I wish I had as much confidence in anything as Mom has in her pot roast.

"I'll make the pitch," I promise, resigned to my fate. I might be able to tell Trevor and Maddy no, but I'm a long way off from being able to say those two terrifying letters to my mom.

There's clinking around on the other side of the line. "Mom?"

"I'm just checking the cupboards. I need to go shopping. I'll have to let you go."

Our dinner is more than a couple of days away, but my mom is going to rush to the store tonight — because I'm bringing a man home for dinner. This isn't going to end well.

* * * *

I've hunkered down in the library, trying to squeeze in a few hours of study time before my social obligations take over my night. My phone buzzes and lights up with the shop number. I smile wide. "Missing me, Big Man?"

"Hello to you too." Rob's light tenor and easy laugh sounds through the phone. *Oops.*

"Sorry, Rob." My cheeks catch fire. "I thought it was Devin."

"So I guessed. Sorry to disappoint you."

"No disappointment. What can I do for you?"

"We're looking to do an inventory tonight. Hoping to validate our new system. Finally silence all those naysayers."

Devin's the last hold-out resisting the new system. Everyone else adores it. Even Mikey, once I showed him the voice input and icon options. Devin was pissed when he found us in the office at the crack of dawn. He was desperate for an explanation, but Mikey's dyslexia is none of Devin's business.

"What time are you starting?" I ask Rob, wondering if I can make it after my dodgeball game.

"We're hoping to start as soon as we close up shop. But whenever you can make it, Jessie. I know you're a busy young lady."

I pull my phone away and check the clock. It's already past four o'clock. The shop closes in less than two hours. *Damn it.* I'd have to cancel my whole night. I toss my head back and shut my eyes. I'd much rather see Devin than any of the stupid other things I'm supposed to be doing.

"Jessie? You still there?" Rob's voice snaps me back to reality.

"I'll be there."

The coward that I am, I type out a text to Maddy and tell her I'm not going to make the game tonight. I stare down at my phone, waiting for the river of sad face emojis to come pouring in. Instead I get—

Don't worry about it. Now that we're in the finals everyone wants to play! Ha. See ya later babe!

Huh. Wasn't expecting that. But that was the easy one. I take a deep breath, dial Hannah's number and gnaw on my bottom lip.

"Hey, Jessie. What's up?" the sweet voice of my sorority's president chirps in my ear.

"Hey, Hannah. So, I hate to do this, but is there any way you could find someone else to host the board game night tonight?" There's a quick pause and the

146

---

awkwardness makes me keep blabbering. "I feel awful, but there's—"

"Hold on a sec," Hannah cuts me off. Another long pause leaves me begging to make excuses. "Okay."

I shake my head. "Okay?"

"Yeah. I just texted Michelle and she said she'd be happy to host. She was going anyway."

"Oh, great. Thanks!"

"Sure thing. Catch you later, Jessie."

The line dies and I hold my phone out in front of me. *That was so easy.* I feel like I have a new superpower. I jog to my car, excited as hell at the new turn my night has taken.

* * * *

I parked fifteen minutes ago, and am still sitting here watching Devin in his element. I thought he'd be out front helping customers, but Rob's got that covered. Instead, Devin's in one of the bays, elbow-deep in a red sedan. His dark hair is slicked back and his strong jaw is locked in place. He looks angry—he has a resting grump-face. The muscles in his forearm flex, making his tattoos dance. He looks menacing. Devious. But he's the opposite. He's steadfast and loyal. Caring and gentle. *And sexy as hell.*

"Jessie!" Rob calls out to me with his booming voice as he comes around the counter to wrap me in his arms. "I feel like I haven't seen you in ages. Where you been keeping yourself?"

A deep grumble draws my eyes over to Devin, standing in the doorway between the shop and the service bays. "She's got better places to be."

He's wiping his hands on a dark rag, not looking at me. Tension wraps the three of us in a tight grip.

Rob clears his throat. "I'm going to tell the guys to wrap it up so we can get to this inventory."

I cock out a hip. "Where could be better than here?"

"You tell me." Devin slips his rag into his back pocket and glares at me. "You're the one staying away."

"I'm just keeping my promise. Isn't that what you want? Me out of your hair?" He shakes his head. My heart skitters to a stop. "You saying you like having me around now?"

He groans. It's his exhausted, frustrated sound. "Wouldn't be my girlfriend if I didn't want you around."

My heart explodes with joy and I smile so wide my face hurts. "Girlfriend?" I ask, taking a step toward him. I bite my lip, beyond excited. "Little old me?"

He nods once, a quick up and down affirmation that he's in this with me. That we're dating.

"Well, as your *girlfriend*, I have to say it wouldn't kill you to call me. Ask me to come around more." I step right up next to him, letting my chest brush against his.

"Told Rob to call you." He drops his hands to my sides and leans down into me. I smell that delicious tangy citrus smell on his skin that makes my ovaries explode, but I'm not done being a brat yet.

"You had your boss call your girlfriend?" He hums a yes in my ear. I circle my arms around him. "And that doesn't seem chickenshit to you?"

He pulls me against him hard and a deep growl rumbles in my chest. A storm brews in my stomach at his possessive touch. He grips my neck and pulls my lips to his, silencing me with the dominant claim. He slides his tongue into my mouth like it's his personal playground. His kisses are demanding and attentive. They say I'm his prized possession. When Devin pulls back, I'm lightheaded and my knees are weak.

"That chickenshit?" he asks in that deep, sultry voice.

I shake my head, not yet regaining my ability to think, much less speak.

Devin stays within arm's reach all night as we count all the different car parts on the back shelves of the shop. He's quiet, but considerate. The hours tick by in an easy rhythm. Every few minutes, he'll touch me, kiss me or hold me. The moments are fleeting, but persistent. I love having him at my side. My phone's buzzing is constant in my pocket, no doubt reminders of the handful of other things I was supposed to be doing tonight. My sorority sisters. My study partners. My dodgeball team. I don't care. For the first time, I'm in no hurry to rush off anywhere.

"You ready to eat your words?" I taunt Devin while he stands behind me at the counter. We've finished entering in all the tallies from our inventory and now it's time to see what kept better track, his hand invoices or my new system.

"Ready to devour something," he croons in my ear. With an arm on either side of me, he surrounds me with his strong body. I wiggle against him and let out a little laugh.

A few clicks later and I'm proven right beyond any arguments. I point at the screen and let out a triumphant, "Ha!"

I slide out of Devin's arms and hop around in a graceful and understated victory dance. Devin sets his hands on his hips and leers at me. Rob pops out from the office with a soft chuckle. "I take it the system works?"

Devin nods and I shout, "Of course it works! Was there ever any doubt?"

Rob and I both glance at Devin. He doesn't say a word, but he slides a giant pile of paper invoices into the trash. That's as close to an acknowledgement of my victory as I am going to get.

"Looks like you'll have a lot more time for that budding personal life, Dev," Rob adds, heading for the door. "I'm gonna leave you kids alone. Enjoy the rest of your evening."

"Night, Rob." I saunter back to the counter and hop up onto it. Grabbing Devin's collar, I pull him between my thighs. "Well, Big Man, I was right."

Devin brushes the hair off my shoulder and drags his lips across my neck.

"But don't worry. I've got a way you can make it up to me for doubting my awesome business sense."

Devin grips my thighs and pulls me to the edge of the counter. I snake my hands between us and push him away.

"Unh-uhh. You don't get a reward for being a brat." I wag a finger at him.

Devin lets out a deep sigh. If he's annoyed now, he's going to be livid in a few seconds when he finds out he's got major boyfriend duties coming his way already.

"You. Me." I point to his chest, then my own, and his eyes light up. "And my family." His eyes go wide in something that looks a bit like panic. "Saturday night for the monthly Allen family dinner."

"You sure?" he asks, his voice soft and hesitant.

"Positive. Momma Allen's orders."

Devin's jaw drops. "You told your mom about me?" He sounds embarrassed and giddy.

I slap my hands on his shoulders. "Technically, I told my brother Jake. And that blabbermouth told Mom."

Devin's excitement slips away. He looks down at the floor and nods. He tries to pull away, but I grip his shirt.

"Hey, where you going?"

"Like you care," is his terse response.

I pull him into me and wrap my legs around him to make damn sure he isn't going anywhere. "Excuse me?" I ask, cupping his face and forcing him to look at me.

"I get it. You're stuck bringing me because your brother can't keep a secret. I'm nothing special."

His expression is hard as a slab of marble, but those eyes... Those deep, dark eyes hold so much uncertainty. I push down the urge to tell this giant teddy bear in his grizzly bear disguise that I love his brooding ass.

I'm not ready to take that leap just yet, so I tell him what the pouty grump needs to hear instead. "Jake, my middle brother, is my best friend. I can tell him anything and he'll give me the hard truth he knows I need to hear. But I've *never* talked to him about guys before. It was this unspoken rule. My love life was my business, but then I guess there's never been anyone worth talking about."

"But you told him about me? Us?" Devin slides his hands up from my knees to my thighs, gripping me firmly. *Possessively.*

I nod. "I asked him if I was coming on too strong. If I was going to get myself hurt."

"And?" Devin asks, his coal-black eyes searching mine.

I take a deep breath and quirk up the corner of my mouth. "He said to stop being such a pussy."

A thick chuckle rumbles out of Devin, making my heart dance. "I think I like Jake."

"Did I mention he's the one who told my mom and got us into this mess?" I groan. "I've *never* brought someone home before. She's been waiting for me to have a serious boyfriend since I hit puberty. I swear, she's registering for wedding china as we speak!"

A full-fledged laugh racks Devin's body and a warmth surges through my veins at the rich sound. He pulls me off the counter, pinning me in place against it. I'm waiting for him to balk at the idea of an Allen family dinner, or the mere mention of the dirty word 'wedding' three dates into our relationship, but he doesn't. Instead, he wraps me in his strong, tattooed arms and kisses me, soft and sweet. Like he's savoring me.

"I'm serious. I've got three brothers and a wedding-crazy mother. You have no idea what you're getting yourself into."

"Stop being such a pussy," Devin quips. He claims me with his full lips again before I can smart off. For the first time, I think I've found something I like more than being a smart ass. Kissing Devin Bennett might be my favorite activity in the world.

Chapter Nineteen

Devin

"Jamie is the baby. He thinks he's the most charming thing on two legs, but he's harmless. Jake is like me only with a penis. You'll *adore* him." Jessie gives me that sassy look that has me falling more in love with her every damn day.

"No doubt," I deadpan. She hits me on the shoulder and I chuckle.

"Jared is the one you have to worry about."

I cock an eyebrow. I'm six-two and weigh two-twenty. I'm not worried about shit.

"I'm serious. He can be an overprotective jerk. He made my prom date break out into hives!"

"I'll be fine." I've met plenty of puffed-up pretty boys in my time and a handful of real shady people. Jessie's three white-collar brothers aren't going to chase me off.

A quick forty-five-minute ride and we're deep in the suburbs. Green lawns, picket fences, waving flags and pert mailboxes as far as the eyes can see. Jessie points to the last house on the corner and I pull up to her parents' place. It looks the same as the hundreds of other cookie-cutter places on this street, except this one's got half a dozen cars crammed in the driveway.

Jessie unbuckles her seatbelt. "You ready for the third degree?"

I tuck a strand of her golden hair behind her ear. "Your brothers don't scare me, JB."

"I was talking about my mom." The corners of her mouth tip up. "Hope you're ready to talk about wedding colors, Big Man."

I swallow hard, feeling like I've got shards of glass stuck in my throat. Jessie climbs out of the car with a laugh. She reaches for my hand as we walk up the long driveway. I tighten my hand around her slender fingers. Her bright purple nail polish puts a smile on my lips.

Jessie stops at the front door, spinning to face me. I step away, caught off guard by the action.

"Too late to turn back now." She makes a cross over her chest. Her eyes are locked on mine when she reaches behind her and opens the door. "Once more unto the breach. Watch your six, Big Man." Mischief dances across her beautiful face.

Stepping across the threshold, I'm assaulted by delicious smells and booming voices. Both get stronger as I follow Jessie farther into the house.

"They don't have the run game. They'll never win a championship without it," a deep voice bellows down the long hallway.

"You don't need a run game when you've got Davis' arm. That guy's a freakin' cannon," a second man's voice chimes in.

"Nah, it's the defense that's gonna keep them out of the top spot," a third voice calls out before all three begin talking over each other in indistinguishable squabbles.

Jessie and I round a corner at the same time, stepping into the large kitchen that seems to house the entire extended Allen family. Every single one of whom goes quiet at the sight of me standing next to Jessie. I swear, even the baby crying just a second ago is silent.

"Hi, everyone," Jessie's warm voice chirps, echoing among the human statues. She side-eyes me with a nervous laugh. "I think you might've broken my family."

I place my hand on her lower back and take a look around the room. Huddled around a bowl of chips and dip are three clean-cut guys. They're carbon copies, identical except for each being a few years younger than the next. Sandy-blond hair, broad shoulders and square jaws. They're harmless enough—I don't bother giving them a second glance. Behind them, leaning against the sink, is a woman with golden-brown skin and long black hair falling down her back in tight curls. She'd be pretty if those brown eyes weren't puffy and red in a way that makes me think she hasn't had a good night's sleep in about a month. Still, she stares down at a little bundle in her arms like it carries all her hopes in this world.

The sound of an oven door closing draws my attention over to a short woman with brown hair muddled with gray. She takes in the room, alarmed by the sudden quiet—a rarity in the Allen clan, I'm guessing. Her gaze follows the path of everyone's to land on me and Jessie frozen in the doorway. A bright smile lights up her face and her green eyes dance with joy. They're identical to the ones that have been haunting my dreams these past few weeks.

"Everyone, this is Devin." Jessie points at me over her shoulder with her thumb. "Devin, this is everyone."

Jessie's brothers all straighten and cross their arms in choreographed unison while her mom claps and squeals. As if on cue, the baby starts crying again. *I've got one fan in this room.* I cross the crowded kitchen and hold out a plate to Jessie's mom.

"Thanks for inviting me, Mrs. Allen." She blushes and giggles. It's the same light sound as Jessie's. I can tell we're going to be fast friends. "My sister made these cookies as a thank you for taking me off her hands for the day."

"Oh, how thoughtful," she gushes. "And please, call me Jenny."

"Jenny," I say with a nod.

"She also made him promise to be on his best behavior," Jessie calls from across the room. I glance at her over my shoulder and she's taken the same stance as her brothers, arms crossed and feet wide. "Don't let the gentleman act fool you. He's insufferable."

"You've met your match then, sis," her middle brother calls out.

"Bite your tongue, Jake," Jenny calls out with a snap of her dish towel. Jessie is less subtle as she charges after him, fists flying. She socks him in the arm, reaching past her other brother to do it. She wags a finger at all three of them.

"Best behavior from the three of you, too!" she demands.

The woman holding the baby snorts. "Not like that's a high bar. Put a pig in a dress…"

"Hey!" The oldest brother objects. He stalks over to the sink and wraps his arms around her, kissing her then the baby on their foreheads. "I'm not a pig. Even if I do look damn good in a dress."

She slaps him in the chest. "Take your son, Miss Piggy." She hands him the little bundle. He snorts into the blankets and the baby stops crying, transfixed by the pig noises.

What the hell kind of crazy-ass family did I get myself mixed up with?

"Ignore them." The woman holds out her hand. "I'm Mariana Allen. Miss Piggy over there is my husband, Jared. And that little booger is our son, Miguel." Despite the bags under them, her eyes sparkle as she stares across the kitchen at her ridiculous husband making an assortment of barn noises to their son, who's giggling in hysterics.

"Devin." I give her hand a firm shake.

"Welcome to the crazy," she adds under her breath.

"Thanks."

Jenny grabs my hand and pulls me out of the kitchen, throwing a "Watch the pot roast," over her shoulder. After a chorus of grumbling, she whips around. "You know the rules. You can help or you can starve."

"What about him?" Jessie's youngest brother pipes up, pointing at me.

"James Benjamin Allen, we do not point fingers in this house." James' finger wilts, his hand dropping to his side. "Devin is our guest. And to make up for being so rude, you just volunteered for dish duty."

Jessie lets out a loud laugh and points at her youngest brother. Jenny's unforgiving gaze falls on her daughter.

"Jessica Bridget Allen. Thank you for volunteering to help your brother."

Jenny grabs hold of my hand again, tugging me out of the kitchen. We're not two steps away when Jessie's soft voice squeaks, "Crap."

Jenny turns to me, her lips in a tight line. "I swear, despite appearances, they weren't raised in a barn."

With flawless timing, Jared belts out an ear-piercing donkey's hee-haw. Mariana and I bust out laughing.

"Oh, for Pete's sake," Jenny sighs, throwing her arms up in defeat.

I follow her into the living room and sit down next to her, where she pats the couch.

"Tell me about yourself, darling."

I clear my throat. I'm a tattooed auto mechanic who barely finished high school. The son of an abusive felon serving twenty years for aggravated assault, his third strike. I'm not the guy a mother picks out for her only daughter. "Not much to tell, ma'am."

Jenny tilts her head. Her face is soft and her features inviting. It's a warmer welcome than I was expecting. *Than I deserve, considering I've been making a point of driving her daughter crazy for the last few weeks.*

"I somehow doubt that," she says. "Tell me about your family. Your parents still together?"

I swallow hard, my hands balling into fists at my sides. "No. My mom ran off a long time ago and my dad's in prison. Will be for the rest of his life, I hope."

Jenny hums with a simple nod. It's acknowledgment without judgment. "Brothers and sisters?"

"A sister, Rebecca. Becs."

"Older or younger?"

"Younger. She's graduating high school this year. Got a bunch of different scholarship offers too. She's smart as hell." Warmth fills my chest, picturing the only decent member of my family.

Jenny leans back, glancing down the hallway. The ruckus continuing from the kitchen confirms we're still alone. "My Jessie Bird sees something in you. And you know, she's special."

I nod and wait, expecting to be told off in the sweetest way.

"She's just like her father. A hummingbird. Beautiful and quick. She thinks if she buzzes around fast enough, nothing can touch her. She doesn't realize how fragile she is. But you and I know life's little secret." Jenny winks at me, despite the fact that I'm confused as hell. "Fast as she might fly, someday she'll need someplace safe to land."

Jenny taps my hand and I let my fists relax. Lacing her fingers with mine, she squeezes and those familiar hazel eyes search mine. "The trick is teaching a free bird the value of a home when all they can see is a cage."

I'm staring at Jenny, trying to wrap my brain around the meaning behind her words.

"Mom?" Jessie's voice calls out down the hallway. I'm still sitting in stunned silence when she comes into view. "What's going on?"

Jenny leans back with a satisfied smile. "Nothing, darling. Just getting to know your love."

Jessie's eyes go wide and snap to mine. "Mom!" she screeches. "I told you — we just started dating. I thought Jared having a kid would buy the rest of us some time."

"Is it a crime to want to see all my children happy?"

"Crime? No. Obnoxious and smothering? Yes."

Jenny holds her hands up. "Just a friendly chat. Right, Devin?"

I nod, shifting my gaze between Jenny and Jessie, who've engaged in some kind of staring contest.

The front door swings wide open and in walks the original Allen, identical to Jessie's brothers although somewhat more weathered.

"I've got the pickles," he calls out in triumph.

Jenny jumps up off the couch and snatches the massive jar of pickles out of his hands. "Thank you, dear. Those will be perfect when we make sandwiches with the leftovers tomorrow."

The man shakes his head. "But I thought —"

"This is Devin, Jessie's new boyfriend," Jenny interrupts him. "Devin, this is my husband, John."

I stand and shake John's hand. *John and Jenny must have one hell of a sense of humor, naming all four kids with J names.*

"Well, I better put these up." Jenny scurries off back to the kitchen.

Jessie elbows her dad in the ribs. "Oooh, you don't even know how close you came to disaster, do you?" she asks.

"Huh?" John is beyond confused.

"You almost let the *secret* ingredient to Mom's famous mac and cheese slip in front of an *outsider*." Jessie jerks her head to me.

"Oh, right. Oops." The two share a chuckle. He kisses Jessie on the forehead. "How have you been, Birdie?"

"Good, thanks. How goes the great kitchen debate?"

Her father groans. "I'll be honest, if I hear the word *chartreuse* one more time, I'm going to go mad. A man can only take so much."

"Fight the good fight, Dad."

The whole family has an easy familiarity. There's a constant buzz throughout the house and dinner is controlled chaos. To Jenny's near-constant horror and despite her best efforts, her children are barely civilized. John seems to revel in it. I'm used to a certain level of crazy. Between my absentee father, foster families and group homes, I've seen my fair share of ridiculousness, but the Allan clan takes the cake. They bring sibling rivalry up a notch.

Jared mocks Jake for not being able to figure out how to pee standing up until he was seven. In defense of her favorite brother, Jessie reminds Jared that he was shitting his pants longer than the rest of them. She even drags Jenny into the battle, confirming how long it took to potty train her oldest son.

Not to be left out, James — Jamie Wamie to his merciless siblings — chooses this moment to mention he was the fastest to get potty trained. *Big mistake, kid.* His three older siblings gang up on the baby of the family, listing off an unending string of things he took the longest to learn. These guys don't forget a thing. And they don't let each other forget a thing either.

It'd be nice to have someone to fight with the way they do. All their bickering is based on an interconnected history and laced with a deep love. Becs gives me shit and Austin is a brother in everything but blood. Still, the connection the Allen siblings have is something else. They share every memory. Every moment, good and bad, they've been there for one another.

It's a hard reminder of how different Jessie and I are, how this is going to end. I should walk out of this dining room now and save us from the destruction that follows me around like a toxic cloud, but I can't force myself to let go. I glance at Jessie beside me, the familiar wide smile on her lips and joy in her eyes. She's never felt so far away. Desperate to touch her, I set my hand on her knee and squeeze, despite the pain of my heart cracking. Without looking, she interlaces our fingers and squeezes back.

I let my attention bounce from one family member to the next, like I'm watching a tennis match on speed.

"I'm the first one to give mom a grandbaby." Jared holds Miguel up as his adorable, drooling trump card. "The only one of us that's made one of these!"

"Oh, you made him, did you? All by yourself?" Mariana deadpans, her lips pursed and her brow furrowed.

"Yeah, you only get half credit. Plus, just 'cause he's the only one we *know of* doesn't mean he's the only one," Jake challenges.

John lets out a long chuckle, but Jenny stares at Jake like she could give him an ass-whooping with just her eyes.

"Jacob Brody Allen! You promise me right now I don't have grandbabies out there I'll never get to meet! I would never forgive you."

Jake's eyes go wide as he chokes on his mashed potatoes and waves his hands in front of him. "Hell no, Mom!"

Jenny gives him a curt nod.

Mariana turns her attention to me, the other outsider. "How about you, Devin?"

"Hmmm?"

"Any kids?"

The room goes dead silent. Seven sets of eyes study my face with an intensity I wasn't prepared for.

I shake my head with a smirk twisting my lips. "None that I know of."

Three heartbeats pass in complete silence. Jake is the first one to crack up. This time the mashed potatoes almost come out of his nose. Jessie is the next to keel over in hysterics, followed by her dad. Jared pounds the table as a deep chuckle rumbles out of him. Mariana laughs into her hand, trying to hide it from Jenny.

"Oh, for Heaven's sake," Jenny sighs with a shake of her head. Her reaction sets off another round of laughter from the Allen clan.

When Jessie catches her breath, she wipes a tear from her eyes and pulls me to her. She kisses me on the cheek and whispers, "I…I'm crazy about you."

The words shoot a burning surge of adrenaline from my chest out to the tips of my fingers and the bottom of my toes. I cup her face and claim her lips.

"That's enough of that," Jared grumbles from across the table.

Jessie sticks her tongue out at him. Under the table, she slides her hand up my thigh and massages the growing thickness there. *Fuck no.* I'm not part of her crazy competition with her siblings. I'm not afraid of her brothers, but I respect them enough not to let their sister give me a handy under the dining room table. I slide my hand under Jessie's, interlocking our fingers and squeezing. She sighs, but squeezes back.

Jenny follows through on her threat, and after dinner Jamie and Jessie sulk off to the kitchen to take care of the dishes. John, Jenny, Jake and Mariana head off into the living room to watch Miguel roll over and other assorted miracles. Jared catches me returning from the bathroom for the conversation I've been waiting all night for.

"Jessie is my baby sister," he starts, his voice firm and cold. His arms are crossed and he's scowling. I'd be a little more intimidated if I didn't know how great his cow impersonations are.

I grunt in affirmation, crossing my arms and matching his scowl.

"Hurt her and we'll fuck you up."

I give him a single nod. I'd tear my own arms off before I intentionally hurt Jessie, but I know there's a devil inside me that I can't always control. I pray to whatever God will listen that she never sees it.

"Good." A wide grin spreads across his face, transforming him again into the goofy dad from earlier. He slaps a hand on my shoulder and adds, "You seem like a decent guy. Hope it lasts. Her attention span is shorter than Miguel's." He chuckles and steps past me, heading into the bathroom.

That makes two family members who felt the need to tell me how inconsistent Jessie is. I wish I could say I was surprised, but I'm not. Still, it stings to realize that even if I'm the one who walks away, she's the one who can move on.

I make my way back to the living room to find Jenny and Mariana on the ground playing with Miguel while John watches from the couch with a proud and protective grandfather's glint in his eye.

John jerks his head to the seat next to him, so I take it.

"Seems like just yesterday my Jessie Bird was that size," he muses.

"What's the story behind the nickname?" I ask.

John lets out a reminiscing sigh and nods to Jake, who's standing in the corner fiddling with his phone. *Swiping right until his finger falls off, from what Jessie says.*

"You can blame that one. When he'd get mad at her, he'd use her full name like their mother does. But poor guy couldn't say Jessica to save his life. Jessica Bridget came out more like Jessie Bird. And the way she's always flying about, it just stuck."

I nod with a light smile. "They're close?" I ask, nodding to Jake.

"Two peas, those two. When Jessie was about ten, she wanted this silly doll with these big eyes. Jake, what was the name of that doll Jessie wanted?"

"Bratz, just like she is," Jake answers without taking his eyes off his phone.

"This is family time, Jacob Brody. Put the phone away or it'll meet my blender." Jenny's sweet voice has Jake shoving his phone back in his pocket. *No idle threat – she's pulverized some electronics before.* I can see where Jessie gets that determination from.

John snaps his fingers. "Bratz! That's it. I never liked 'em. Thing gave me the willies. But she spent months begging us for that silly thing. Promising good grades and a clean room. Anything and everything. She even talked that one" – John points over to Jake – "into a crazy scheme." John chuckles and Jake sighs. "Going door to door, they told all the neighbors they were collecting for kids in need." John slaps his thigh with a hearty laugh.

"Mom lost her mind. Chewed my ass so hard some of it's still growing back. We went door to door again, returning the money and apologizing." Jake sinks down on the couch next to his dad. "We spent *weeks* saving. Extra chores, lemonade stands and saving our allowance. And after all that, she played with the damn thing for a day and tossed it!"

"Language," Jenny snaps, her hands covering Miguel's little ears. She side-eyes me. "It was longer than that."

"A week. Tops. She's a stubborn brat when you tell her she can't have something, but once she gets it...pffft." He scoffs. "Nothing keeps Jessie Bird interested for long."

That makes three. Jessie's entire family seems to think she's incapable of caring about much for long. These people know her, inside and out. They love her unconditionally, that much is clear. But even they don't suffer any illusions about how fast she'll move on.

I lean back into my chair and let it all settle in. Jessie is all about the chase. My first instinct was right about her — she's not in anything for the long haul. She just likes shaking shit up and disappearing. *Fine. We can do that, Jessie Bird. I'll get mine and get out before you have a chance to be bored.*

Chapter Twenty

Jessie

My dad clears his throat behind me while Jamie's drying off the last of the pots and I'm filling up the dishwasher.

"About done?" he asks.

"Just about," Jamie answers.

Dad grabs an extra dishrag off the counter and takes the pan from Jamie. "I'll finish up," he says.

"Yes!" my little brother shouts, escaping out of the kitchen faster than a flash of lightning.

"Hey! Why does he get an early release?" I pout, shutting the dishwasher.

Dad keeps his eyes focused on the dish in front of him. "Because I want to talk to my favorite daughter."

"Your only daughter."

"Which is why it'd be bad if you weren't my favorite," he jokes.

I chuckle, picking up Jamie's discarded dishrag and drying off a saucepan. I gesture to the living room. "Devin surviving out there?"

Dad nods. "He was alive when I left."

"Good. I prefer to keep him that way."

"Something tells me he's seen worse than your brothers."

I nod. "He hasn't had it easy, but I think that just means he appreciates what he has more."

"People who don't have much usually do. He seems to care about you quite a bit."

My heart flips in my chest. "You think so?"

"I do. He'd have to, to put up with your mother." A moment of silence passes between us before Dad clears his throat. "So, is that the plan? To keep him?"

I shoot away from Dad and buzz around the kitchen, wiping down every surface a dozen times. "I don't know."

"Don't you?"

I bite my lip and shrug. Dad doesn't say anything more as we put away the last of the clean dishes and utensils. Our work done, I stand and stare off at the empty doorway. Light voices drift in from the living room. I can't make out Devin's gruff baritone, but I know he's there. Sitting with my family, listening to my most embarrassing childhood stories and laughing, no doubt. The thought has a comforting warmth, radiating from my chest and tingling down all my limbs.

We make our way down the long hall, the sound of laughter getting louder as we get closer. I catch a glimpse of Devin, smiling wide and bouncing baby Miguel on his knee. I reach out to brace myself on the wall as my heart shatters. I've never had a biological clock, but the sight of Devin's toned and tattooed arm wrapped around a drooling bundle of cuteness starts a countdown in my womb.

"Dad?" I turn to face him behind me.

"Yeah, kiddo?"

"Do you think you can fall in love in a month?" I ask, feeling my cheeks catch fire.

He gives me that knowing *Dad* look, the one that reminds me he's older and wiser. He tucks a strand of hair behind my ear and cups my face.

"Jessie Bird, you can fall in love in a single moment. I did with your mother."

I spin on my heels and watch Devin. I know deep in my heart that my dad's right.

So it turns out I'm not just in love with Devin, but I'm also desperate to have his babies. Not like tomorrow, but some day. And I'm terrified. I have no idea if he feels the same.

Most guys are pretty obvious with how they feel about me. They're just there, easy for me to reach out and claim if I wanted to. But the only guy I want to claim is Devin, and he seems to like me against his will. He fights it with every ounce of strength he has, and that's a lot. He's all muscle.

He likes me, but it also seems he resents me for it. Like I'm a weight around his shoulders. In the beginning, it didn't bother me. It was a game and I love a challenge. Before there wasn't any risk. Now it seems like everything is on the line. It was a lot more fun trying to steal his heart before he stole mine. He can hurt me now. It'd be easy. All he'd have to do is walk away.

He's been quiet since we left my parents' house. No shocker there—he's always quiet, but I don't have it in me to fill the silence with my usual nonsense. The classic rock station playing on the radio is the only sound in the car as we drive to my sorority house.

Devin parks and follows me up the steps to my door. I pull out my keys and fiddle with them.

"Looks like you survived my brothers unscathed."

"No hives," he deadpans. He's always gruff, but there's a stronger bite to his remark than usual. I'm used to the annoyed lilt to his voice, but now there's an indifference to his words that's never been there before.

I bite my lip, nervous yet desperate to ask him inside. He stands stoic on my porch, waiting for me to do something. *Say something.* All my usual sassiness has deserted me. I don't want to put on a show. I want him to see me.

I step into him, placing my hand over his heart as I look up into those dark eyes. "Thanks for today." My voice is soft. *Small.* It doesn't sound like me.

Devin's grunt is his only response. He doesn't wrap his arms around me. He doesn't pull me into him. He doesn't kiss me. He's slipping away. I glance between the front door and his chest.

I steel myself. "Want to come in?"

A beat of silence is broken by his possessive growl. He leans down and claims my mouth. I snake my arms around his neck and he moans against my lips. There's a fervor there, a need brewing between us stronger than any I've ever felt. With our lips still locked together, I reach behind me and open the door, pulling him in with me before closing and locking it.

I pull back and he glares down at me. We don't say a word, but there's a silent acknowledgment. I slide my hand to his before spinning and leading him to my bedroom.

I cross to my nightstand, flicking on the dim light. At the soft click of Devin locking my bedroom door, I pull my shirt off and glance over my shoulder at him. In a breath, he's across the room, wrapping me in those strong arms, his lips devouring the soft skin on my neck.

His grip is hard, his touch demanding. He is rough with my body, like he's desperate for these punishing touches. I melt under his fingertips, every inch of my skin aching for his attention.

"Devin." I call his name on a breathy moan. He shoves me down onto my bed. I bounce off the mattress, stunned by his sudden ferocity.

He tilts his chin at me, his face cold as stone. "Take your clothes off," he commands.

My mouth drops open. "What?" I ask, confused by his distance and hostility. He wants me. He can't kiss me the way he does and not be desperate for me the same way I am for him. But something is wrong. It's like I'm twisting a knife in his back every time he touches me.

He pulls his shirt off over his head, tossing it aside without a care. My eyes drink in his bare chest, tan and chiseled. I'm frantic to run my hands over his smooth skin.

"You heard me." His voice is unforgiving as he rubs the growing bulge in his pants.

His intentions are clear. I want to make love. He wants to fuck. It's a slice to my heart, but I'm ashamed to say I'll take whatever he'll give me. Pushing up to my knees on the bed, I keep his eyes focused on me as I unbutton my pants, teasing him and drawing out my time with him as much as possible.

"Condom?" he barks.

I bite my lip and point to my desk. "Bottom drawer." I blow out a deep breath, sinking down onto my heels. Deflated, I drop my eyes to my lap.

There's a loud rustling as he searches the drawer, followed by a stark silence. I snap my eyes to him. He's holding up an old doll, staring at it like it has no place in a grown woman's room. Because it doesn't. It's juvenile and silly, but it's special to me.

"Still play with dolls?" he asks, his voice soft despite mocking me.

I shoot off the bed and snatch the Bratz doll out of his hands, shoving it into the drawer instead of returning her to her normal place, perched on the corner of my desk. I grab a condom, slap it into his bare chest and shut the drawer with a loud thud.

"No." My answer is sharp as a razor, meant to slash at him the way he's cut me. He clasps a hand over mine, curling it around my fingers and squeezing. His gaze burns into me, begging for an explanation. The sincerity there disarms me. I suck in a quick breath, worried I may not be able to take another under his piercing eyes.

"That's Sasha. She has sentimental value. Where I go, she goes."

"Didn't think you were the sentimental type, JB," Devin croons. He cups my face in a gentle caress. He strokes a featherlight touch along my cheek with his thumb.

"I'm full of surprises, Big Man."

He tilts his head and searches my features for something. I have no idea what, but he seems to find it. His full lips turn up into a small smile and his studious gaze turns adoring.

"You sure are." He leans down and his mouth finds mine, devouring me with gentle but steadfast kisses. He smooths his hands over my body in reverent, worshiping touches.

I moan his name again and he rewards me with a deep groan. He drops his firm hands to my thighs and lifts me up. He wraps my legs around his trim waist and carries me back to the bed. This time he lays me down gently, not letting me go. He climbs on top, settling between my legs.

He kisses a wet trail down my neck, stalling at my chest. He slides my bra straps off my shoulders with his nimble fingers and I reach behind me to unhook it. He peels it off me, letting the delicate lace drag across my sensitive nipples. I squirm under him at the teasing sensation. He claims one nipple with his hot mouth and the other with his cool hand. Devin Bennett is hot and cold, a beautiful contradiction.

Without releasing my breasts, he slides his other hand between us and finishes unbuttoning my jeans. He eases them down my thighs, leaving me in nothing but my lace panties. He moves down my body, kissing and sucking along the way. Reaching my stomach, he dips his tongue into me, swirling it around the thick bar of my belly button piercing. *Holy shit.* Who knew my stomach was directly connected to my vagina? He flicks his tongue over the steel, tickling the hypersensitive skin around the piercing, and my clit pulses with need.

"Lower," I plead. He obliges.

He hooks the side of my lace panties, slides them gingerly down my thighs and tucks them into his pocket. He rises to his knees, taking in my naked body.

I drag a hand over my pert nipple and revel in the desire burning in those coal-black eyes.

"Exquisite," he moans.

I lean forward and tug open his pants. He doesn't move. I slide my hand into them, realizing he's not wearing boxers at the feel of his hot, hard length filling my palm. My eyes flutter shut and I suck my bottom lip into my mouth, biting down when he gets harder in my grip.

On a pained exhale he calls out, "Jessie."

I love the sound of my name on his lips, raspy and pleading. I open my eyes to see his head drop back with pleasure, mouth agape and fists balling at his side. He's hard as stone, but the big man is putty in my hands.

"Take your clothes off," I simper.

A devilish grin tickles his beautiful mouth as he slides off the bed. I prop myself up on my elbows and watch with rapt attention as he hooks his thumbs into his pants and slides them down to his ankles before kicking them aside. His cock stands proud, surging up to his stomach. He strokes it and I lick my lips, eager for the taste of him.

I crawl towards him and take his length down my throat without preamble. I cup his balls, rolling them under my fingers with gentle pressure.

"Fuck," he mumbles, sliding a hand into my hair. He guides my pace, slowing me to an agonizing rhythm. His balls tighten in my hand and he's close to coming when he pulls away from me. I whimper, amazed at his restraint, but dissatisfied not to have finished.

He pushes me onto my back before flipping me onto my stomach and lifting my hips. It's decisive, but not rough. I'm spread out before him, waiting for him to plunge into me, when a cool breath hits my burning-hot sex. The sensation sends a shudder through my entire body. I'm still shaking when he pushes his thick tongue into me. He grabs my ass with one hand, spreading me for him while he strokes my slick folds and teases my clit with the other. The little bundle of nerves screams with joy. He rubs lazy circles with his fingertips and he fucks me with his tongue. The comforter drags across my nipples as I rock into him. A familiar tightness coils in my stomach, warning of imminent pleasure that might rip me apart. I try to pull away, the sensation too much, but Devin's grip on me is too tight. He keeps my ass pressed against his face as he consumes me.

It starts slow, like a pot beginning to boil, the bubbles rolling over every inch of my body. I feel everything, every tiny sensation. The friction of the bed underneath me. The sheets clenched in my hands. Devin's tongue inside me. His hot breath on my ass. His fingers stroking my clit. A slow boil, building and building, until it spills over in a raging explosion. I scream his name, delirious in complete pleasure. Every muscle in my body constricts and releases over and over until I collapse forward on the bed, exhausted beyond measure. My eyes close and I nearly pass out. My chest heaves and I pant, convinced my heart will never beat a normal rhythm again.

Devin moves up my body, caressing overstimulated skin with those delicious lips, eliciting a moan with every kiss. He reaches for the nightstand and tears open the condom wrapper. I'm filled with a selfish guilt. I'm too spent to repay the favor, but Devin doesn't seem to mind.

He settles behind me, sliding an arm under my head and wrapping it around my shoulders. He rolls me onto my side and holds me against him. His cock presses against the back of my thigh and I pull my leg up toward me, opening myself up for him. Devin grips my hip and slides into me in a lazy stroke. He's unhurried, like he has the rest of his life to make love to me. He kisses my temple as he slides out of me. The gentleness is what I want. What I need. I feel desired. Adored. *Loved.*

I shut my eyes against the tears threatening to spill over. My hand finds his at my collarbone and I intertwine our fingers, squeezing with everything I have. He squeezes back as he slides into me with heavenly ease.

He moves his hand up to my chest, holding me and kissing my neck. He's hugging me to his chest as he makes tender love to me. Devin glides his hand between my legs and my second orgasm catches me by surprise. There is no build up, just a quick and stunning jolt of pleasure radiating through my whole body. As the release reverberates through me, his pace quickens and he comes inside me, his shaky breath in my ear.

He doesn't pull out or away. He keeps me locked in his arms, continuing with his slow, penetrating thrusts for another few moments, like he's not quite ready for our first time to be over. He slides out of me and rolls over long enough to take off the condom and throw it into the trash by my desk. Then he's at my back again, pulling me into him. I fall asleep, wrapped in those tattooed arms.

Chapter Twenty-One

Devin

"Do I get to say I told you so?" Austin asks, leaning against my counter.

I don't look at his smirking ass, keeping my eyes locked on the computer screen. "Not if you want to keep that face lookin' so pretty," I warn him.

He laughs and tells me anyway, making obnoxious kissing noises. I groan and focus on the shop's schedule for the day. I didn't say shit, but sometime in the past couple of weeks, Jessie told Elizabeth we're together. *I think Jessie's told fucking everyone. She might as well buy a fucking billboard to announce that shit.* Elizabeth told Austin, and now the prick is even more annoying than usual.

"Why are you here?" I ask when he slips around to my side of the counter.

"Waiting on Elizabeth." He thumbs through a parts catalog with zero interest.

I snatch it out of his hands and return it to the shelf under the counter where it belongs. "Your girlfriend's not here."

"No shit. Jessie took her out shopping for her birthday. I'm meeting them here to grab some dinner."

I turn to face him. "Whose birthday? Elizabeth's or Jessie's?"

"Tsk. Tsk. You didn't know it's Jessie's birthday? You are a *shit* boyfriend, boyfriend!"

"How was I supposed to know? She didn't say anything."

"Did you ask?"

I shake my head and turn to the computer. "One serious relationship and you're an expert now?"

"I'm a quick study when it matters." He's an idiot. But he's also right.

It's been a long time since I've been with someone who matters to me as much as JB does. It hasn't escaped my notice that JB could also stand for Jessica Bennett. It's crazy to think like that, like maybe someday she'll be my wife, but I can't help it. It's how I am. If I've got something good going, I look for a way to make it permanent. Keep it. And this thing with Jessie isn't good, it's fucking amazing. Even the thought of that bright smile and sunshine hair makes me grin like an idiot.

"What time are they supposed to come by?"

"Jessie didn't say?"

I let out an irritated sigh. "I don't keep tabs on her. She drops by whenever she wants."

I glare at him until he answers. "About six."

I pull out my phone and check the time. Five past four. I've got less than two hours to figure out the perfect gift for her.

"Sean!" I shout into the bays.

He pops over with a "What's up, Boss?"

"Watch the counter. I'll be back before six."

"Got it." He gives me a thumbs up and slides behind the counter.

"I can watch it for you," Austin offers.

I snatch my keys off my desk in the back and crook a finger at him. "You're coming with me, Dr. Strangelove."

He shakes his head in disappointment. "You're using that reference wrong."

"What reference?" I ask.

"Dr. Strangelove. The movie?"

Ever since Elizabeth, he's not only a relationship expert, but an old movie critic too.

"You've never seen it?" he asks, shocked. I shake my head. "Man, it's hilarious. We shou —"

"Later," I cut him off. "We've got a job to do now."

"Yes, boss!" he jeers, following me out of the shop with a mocking militant stomping of his feet.

After he watched the shop for me, I let Sean go. I've closed everything up, rolled down the big bay doors and cleaned up everything except the car I'm working on. I'm the last one in the shop, except Austin, who's still waiting on Elizabeth. He's a pain in the ass, but I'm glad he was around to help me out today. He let me eliminate a dozen gift ideas, like *every* suggestion he had. The top of his list? A vibrator. *What the actual fuck?*

Granted, I had a few shit ideas myself. Top of my list? Sweatpants. Girls like being comfortable. Made sense at the time. Austin vetoed that one pretty quick.

I'm nearly done changing an alternator with Austin pretending to help when he shoots up and dashes off. He hits Elizabeth like a love-seeking missile, wrapping her in a bear hug and swinging the tiny woman around like a crazed lunatic. Elizabeth's giggles make me think it's a regular occurrence.

I wipe off my hands with the rag in my pocket and watch Jessie stroll up to me with those irresistible legs. She slips her arms around my neck and places a kiss on my cheek.

"Hey there, Big Man," she simpers.

I take a deep breath, the smell of her overtaking me. The shop smell fades to the soft scent of cookies, sweet and delicious. I tuck the rag back in my pocket before cupping her face in my hands and kissing the ever-loving shit out of her. I'm starving for this woman.

"Hey there, JB." I place a quick kiss on the tip of her perfect nose.

"We're out," Austin calls to us as he guides Elizabeth out to the parking lot. She gives us a quick wave, tucked into Austin's side. "Happy birthday, Jessie."

"Thanks."

I frown at the reminder that Austin and Elizabeth both know shit about my girlfriend I don't. I turn away from her and return to work. She leans against the grill and stares down at me.

"Well?" she asks.

"Well what?" I call from under the hood.

"Well, are you going to wish me happy birthday?" She slaps me on the ass and I have to bite back a laugh.

"Might. If you'd bothered to tell me it *was* your birthday." I let my annoyance seep through.

I reach for a crescent wrench, but she snatches it before I can. I straighten up and grab for it, but she slides it behind her as quick as can be.

"Jessie..." I growl.

"Devin..." she cajoles. "Talk to me."

I shift her hips and pin her against the car. Her eyes dance with lust. She likes it when I'm handsy. I glare down at her, my grip on her tight and possessive.

"You're mad at me!" She's more surprised than angry. She rests her hand on the familiar spot on my chest. "On my birthday?"

I let out a sharp breath. "Which I had to find out from Austin instead of my girlfriend."

"Oh."

"Yeah. *Oh*."

"You could've asked."

"I shouldn't have to ask. If something is going on with *my* girlfriend, *she* should tell me."

Her head lists to the side. "I wasn't trying to keep a secret. I just didn't want to make a big deal out of it."

I grunt an acknowledgement. I get downplaying it, but she still should've told me. "You told Elizabeth."

"No. I didn't. She was there when my crazy family conference called to sing me happy birthday. The full extended version with Jamie screeching 'and many more' over and over until Mom told him to hush."

My glare eases as a grin breaks through my irritation. I nod and give her a soft kiss, accepting the proffered excuse.

"I'm an open book." She throws her arms wide. "Want to know something, Big Man? Just ask."

I peer down at her. "What do you want for your birthday?"

"To hear you call me your girlfriend over and over again." She winks at me. I shake my head, my grin giving way to a full-on smile.

I pull her forward, slam the hood of the car shut and set her down on top of it. Wrapping one arm around her waist, I pull her to the edge and step between her thighs. I brush her golden hair off her shoulder with my other hand, trailing my nose along her neck.

"Is that all you want, *girlfriend*?" I ask on a breathy exhale.

Jessie wraps her arms around my neck, slipping her fingers into my hair.

"That's not *all* I want." She pulls back and kisses me, dancing her tempting lips over mine.

With her real present burning a hole in my pocket, it's my turn to pull away. She lets out an annoyed moan in disapproval of my breaking the kiss.

"I got you something," I stammer, nervous as fuck that she isn't going to like it.

She leans away, her hazel eyes going wide and her mouth falling open. "You got me a birthday present?"

"Nothing special."

"Can I have it?"

"Now?" I look around the grungy garage.

She grabs my shirt collar, pulling me down to her until our foreheads are touching. "Give it to me, Big Man," she croons.

My grip on her thighs tightens, digging my fingers into her soft skin with need. I cup her face with my left hand, kissing her hard while I grab the velvet box out of my pocket with my right. She blinks, shaking off the lust-filled haze, before her eyes focus on the little box I'm holding between us.

"Devin…" she whispers, tracing the outline of the box in my palm. She cracks it and silence falls on us like a guillotine. Her face is blank, and she's caressing the gold pendant with her delicate fingers.

I swallow the boulder lodged in my throat. "You lost your necklace a couple of weeks ago." I explain, feeling stupid.

"It's a hummingbird."

"Your mom called you a hummingbird. At dinner. Because you never sit still."

She stares at the pendant, silent as the grave. *I should've gone with the damn sweatpants.*

"If you hate it—"

"Shut up," she commands. She grabs my shirt, dragging me down and crushing her lips against mine. Her voice cracks. "I love it."

She snags the pendant and clasps it around her neck in one quick motion.

"How does it look?" she asks, centering the pendant on the chain.

I nod.

"It's perfect," she answers her own question. "You're perfect." She wraps her legs around my hips and pulls me down onto the hood with her.

She slips her hands under my shirt, lifting it up and off, before she throws it away without a care. She repeats the same with her own shirt, her bra following behind it. Cupping her breasts, I bend forward to flick her perky nipples with my tongue. She arches her back into me.

"You want me to fuck you on this Toyota, girlfriend?" I tease.

She nods, biting her lip. "It's a classic."

I let out a low chuckle as I move my hands down to her jeans. Popping the button and slipping them off her impossibly long legs, I quip, "You're a classic."

She's wearing the same bright red boy shorts that tortured my dreams for weeks after she flashed me. I let out a low growl, sliding her panties off and slipping them into my pocket. I'm starting a collection.

Jessie's naked and spread out on the hood of a car. I've never seen anything so fucking sexy in my life. My dick is suffocating in my pants, desperate for a deep breath of Jessie's pussy. My cock can wait. My birthday girl's going to get hers first.

I lean forward and dive into her wet pussy like a man on fire, my mouth claiming her clit without warning or mercy. She fists my hair, tugging at me when I fill her with two fingers. She comes apart fast and hard, alternating between pants and moans.

"You. Inside me. Now," she demands.

"Yes, girlfriend."

Her syrupy laugh coats me with a warm, thick desire. I pull her off the hood and flip her onto her stomach. The car is the perfect height. I grab my wallet out of my back pocket before letting my pants fall to the ground. I whip it open, only to realize I used my spare condom when we fucked in the back seat of my car last week.

"Fuck," I mutter in utter frustration.

Her body still sprawled out on the hood, tempting ass in the air, Jessie turns her face to me. "What's wrong?"

"No condom."

A wicked twinkle dances across her hazel eyes. "I'm on the pill."

I cock my head to the side. "You sure?"

Jessie nods. "Take me, Big Man."

Before she finishes, I'm balls-deep inside her, aching for the connection. I brace myself on the hood, a palm on either side of her body, caging her in. I stay buried inside her, kissing her shoulder blade before slowly pulling out. Jessie whimpers under me, desperate for a faster pace, but I'm going to take my time with her.

I kiss her neck, her back, her shoulder, as I fuck her slow.

"Devin, please," she begs.

"Hmm?" I feign ignorance.

"Faster. Harder."

A smile slides across my face. I lean back and take a tight grip on her slender hips. I pound into her with every punishing thrust.

"Oh God, yes," she moans.

I take her hard, my sweet little hummingbird begging me for more until she shudders with pleasure underneath me. I slow my pace, debating coming inside her. I *want* to come inside of her. Desperately. But I shouldn't. The pill is only effective if she's using it right. I'm trusting her not to have my kid. My heart surges at the idea of my baby inside her. I *want* her to have my kids. Not now, but some day. My brain is still trying to make sense of my heart's declaration when my cock gives up waiting and makes the decision on its own. I come inside Jessie, pleasure racking my body while my heart drowns in a future I'm scared to hope for.

After owning my body on the hood of some complete stranger's car, Devin insisted I come home with him. He wanted to cook me dinner, claiming it was the boyfriend thing to do. I'm supposed to be at a Freshman mixer, but I didn't fight very hard when Devin suggested it. Okay, I didn't fight him at all. A quiet, private dinner with Devin was the perfect way to spend the rest of my birthday. Plus, the mind-blowing, thigh-quivering, soul-shattering sex isn't bad either.

I go limp and collapse, Devin's massive body pressing me down into his bed with a delicious pressure. My arms are pinned between us and I couldn't move if my life depended on it. Good thing I wouldn't want to move even *if* my life depended on it. This must be how swaddled babies feel, tucked in warm security and love. Devin's breath is fast and ragged in my ear. I could almost swear the satisfied three-syllable grunt he lets out is his way of saying *I love you*. I close my eyes and soak in the feel of his warm body and his citrus scent.

He places a soft kiss on my collarbone, a sweet reminder that while he just fucked me like an animal, he's a softie underneath all those tattoos and scowls. I hum at the tingle it shoots straight to my heart.

"Am I crushing you?" he asks, lifting himself up onto his elbow.

I snake my arms around his waist. "In the best way."

He chuckles, kisses my nose and heads to the bathroom. I scoot up the bed, half reclining in a massive pile of pillows. The rest of his tiny apartment is clean and minimalist. *What else was I expecting from Mr. OCD?* But his bedroom is a little sanctuary. A soft pillow oasis. His apartment is just like him, sharp edges and hard lines on the outside, with a warm and cozy center.

He struts back from the bathroom, naked, and flops down on his stomach next to me. His head is in my lap and he grips my ribs, thumbing the exposed skin at the side of my breast.

I run one hand through his thick black hair and rub long strokes up and down his back with the other. His contented sigh lets me know he's appreciative. I don't know what I like more, fighting with him, having sex with him, or this. The quiet moment stretches out and we're both content to just be. It's one of the rare times that I'm living in the moment instead of thinking about what's next.

I trace my fingers over his shoulder blade and still at the long, thick scar there. I've never noticed it before. I probe the white skin with gentle care. It's long since healed.

"My Pops clipped me." Devin's voice turns cold and his body tenses against me.

I pause, my palm covering the old wound. "Clipped you? With what?"

"Vodka bottle."

I pull him tighter against me, a possessive protectiveness surging through me. "Where was your mom?" I bite out, seething. Devin shrugs with his head in my lap, his breathing slow and even.

"Gone."

"Gone?" I ask, but don't give him time to answer. "And she left you with a violent drunk?" *I'd like to get my hands on that guy.*

Devin pulls back, then, rolling to his side, he props his head up on his hand and peers up at me. "That violent drunk was — is — my father."

"And an asshole." I blow an angry breath out through my nose and cross my arms.

"No argument here. Sometimes shitty things happen to good people. That's life." He doesn't sound bitter. He sounds indifferent, and somehow his acceptance is more heart-wrenching.

He peels the sheet down and trails kisses from my side to my belly button. I grab a fistful of his hair with a moan when he flicks my piercing with that dangerous tongue. I'm drowning in lust.

"I bet you still wish on shooting stars," he teases.

"And you don't?"

He looks up, those dark eyes consuming me. I pull in a ragged breath.

"I gave up wishing for shit a long time ago. You want something, you fight for it." In one swift move he seals his lips on mine, our tongues dipping and swirling. He cups my face in a firm but comforting hold. Devin's kiss is everything.

A confession. A claim. A promise.

I drink it in, wishing desperately to make this moment last forever.

He rolls us over, hugging me to his chest. "Go to sleep," he commands. And within minutes I do. Trapped in Devin's arms, I never want to escape.

Chapter Twenty-Two

Devin

My alarm goes off at six, as usual. This time, I hit Snooze and pull Jessie in against me. She's a million degrees, her hot naked body burning into mine. She wiggles her ass against my morning wood and I growl into her sunshine hair.

"Morning, Big Man." Her sleepy voice is sexy as hell.

I cop a feel when Jessie stretches her long, curvy body. She giggles and slaps my hand away. "No time. I'm gonna grab a quick shower. I reek of sex."

I nod. She grabs a pillow and smacks me on the hip. "Go make coffee."

She's in the bathroom with the door closed before I can object. We fucked three times yesterday and I'm ready for round four. I sit on the edge of the bed and listen to her loud, off-key singing. I chuckle, picturing her using a shampoo bottle as a microphone. I'm eager to jump into that shower with her, but the doorknob won't budge.

"Naughty boy," she chides behind the locked door. I pound on it with a groan. "Coooooffeeeee!" Giving up, I get dressed and stomp to the kitchen as instructed.

I'm on my second cup of coffee, sitting at my two-person dining room table, when the unmistakable sound of a Jessie tornado echoes from the bedroom. She's talking to herself now, rambling off a long list of things that she's supposed to do today like she'll forget if she doesn't repeat her schedule out loud.

She struts into the living room in her jeans from last night and one of my shop T-shirts tied in a knot at her side. It's cute as fuck. I watch her storm into the kitchen, opening and closing every cabinet until she finds a mug instead of asking me where they are.

"Coffee cup," she mumbles to herself. "Spoon. Sugar. Milk." She names each item she's looking for, buzzing around my kitchen in a blur of unbridled energy. Finally satisfied, she slips around the counter and heads to the table.

The mug is perched at her lips and her butt almost hits the chair beside me before she shoots up. "Eggs," she says. She skirts by me, her coffee forgotten on the table as she restarts her busy fussing in the kitchen. I stalk up behind her, lift her up and carry her to the table. I settle her into my lap, locking her against me despite her squirming.

"I was going to make breakfast," she whines.

I shake my head, handing her the coffee mug.

"Sit still and drink your coffee." She crosses her arms and glares at me. I let out a long sigh. "Just take a breath. I want five minutes of peace to enjoy my first morning with my girlfriend." I kiss her cheek and nuzzle against her neck until she finally relents.

"Fine. Five minutes." She relaxes into me and we drink our coffee together in blissful silence. "This is nice." I grunt in acknowledgment.

She lets out a long, happy sigh, then downs her coffee and pops up with the indomitable spirit of the first daisy in spring. She steps between my thighs, kicking my knees out wider. One hand on her hip and the other palm up, right in front of my face, she demands, "Now, give me my panties back. I've got places to be."

I keep my eyes locked on her, take a slow sip of coffee and smirk. "No."

Both hands are on her hips now. "Yes," she says, her tone stern.

"No."

"Yes!" She narrows her eyes and purses her lips in mock indignation.

I set down my coffee and interlock my fingers behind my head. I cock an eyebrow and repeat, "No."

She crosses her arms, trying to maintain a frown while a playful grin emerges on those pink lips. "Why are you obsessed with the word no? It makes up half of your vocabulary."

I wrap my arms around her and pull her down into my lap again. I take a deep breath, her usual sweet vanilla scent replaced by the smell of my soap and the lingering hint of sex. "Maybe I like making you scream yes."

She slaps my chest with a soft chuckle. She drops her forehead to mine, shaking it. "You're such an animal! I can't believe I'm in love with you."

Every muscle in my body tenses. I turn to a lump of cement. *What the fuck did she just say?* She lets out a gasp when my arms tighten around her.

"Holy shit. I said that out loud this time, didn't I?" She leans back, shooting her hands up to her mouth and clamping down like she's afraid of what else might come pouring out.

My heart's raging in my chest, trying to break out. *Break free.* I lock my jaw and breathe quick, shallow breaths in and out through my nose.

"This time?" I ask, not easing the death grip I have on her body despite her trying to pull away.

"Don't freak out." She holds her hands up in surrender. "I know it's too early to use the *L-word*. So, I say it in my head instead."

My voice is sharp from the adrenaline surging through every inch of my body. "Since when?"

Jessie bites her bottom lip and looks away, staring at the empty wall over my shoulder. "Since...a while. Does it matter?"

I growl and tighten my arms around her.

"Urgh. Fine. Since our second date." She tilts her head to the side and studies my face. "Although, I think I've been a little bit in love with you since that first kiss."

Someone put those defibrillator paddles to my chest and yell Clear! My heart stops. No warning. It just up and stops beating. My arms drop to my sides and she stands. My head falls back against the chair and I stare up at the ceiling. My gaze goes blurry and I blink a dozen times. My brain reboots, restarting my heart, and I breathe again. I take it all in. *She fucking loves me.* I'm so happy that if she cut me, I'd bleed sunshine and rainbows. If I could bottle this feeling, it'd sell better than cocaine and Prozac combined. An amazed snort escapes my throat.

"Well?" she asks.

I snap my head up and I take her in. She's standing a few feet away, arms crossed, foot tapping. I cock an eyebrow and stare at her, too. "Aren't you going to say it back?"

"No."

"Excuse me?" Her voice goes up about twelve octaves. Her arms drop to her sides at the same time as her mouth falls open. "I just told you I'm in love with you."

"I heard." I smile at her — a full, unabridged, kid-on-their-first-rollercoaster-excited smile.

"And you're not going to say it back?" she asks, as if I just told her I was going to grow wings and fly to Mars.

"No."

"I'm starting to understand why your name rhymes with devil!" I look down at the floor and laugh. This woman is unbelievable. Her false bravado begins to crack and her upper lip quivers. "So, you *don't* love me?" I open my mouth to answer, but she holds up a finger. "If you say 'No,' so help me —"

"Wasn't gonna."

"So you *do* love me?"

"What do you think?" I smile at this beautiful tornado.

She glares at me. "I think you're head over heels, Big Man."

I scoot my chair back, prop my feet up on the table and recline as far as I can. We both glance at my bare feet, a few inches above my head. I wiggle my toes for added emphasis.

"Then just say it!" she screeches.

A devilish grin twists my lips. "No."

"Why the hell not?" she asks on a long whine.

"You deserve better."

She shakes her head, confused. I stand and reach out for her. She takes a step away, but I grab her wrist. I lean against the table, pulling her body up against mine. It's just enough to make up the height difference between us so we're eye to eye.

"You deserve more than some half-assed regurgitated *you too*. When I tell you that I love you — " I pause, letting her take in the words. "It's going to be spontaneous and genuine. You're going to know I'm not saying it to be nice or sweet or any reason other than in that moment I'm completely fucking shattered by how much I love you."

I slip my hand into her hair and smash my lips to hers. I kiss her as hard as I did that first night. The night she fell in love with me. And I fell for her. I kiss her until she gives in, until she melts into me and we become one tangled mess. I kiss her until I don't know where she starts and I end. She places her hand on my chest, her palm finding my heart, and it beats just for her.

She breaks the kiss. "Fine." She pecks me on the mouth and pushes off my chest. With a hair toss, she adds, "But don't take too long. You'll give me a complex!"

Chapter Twenty-Three

Jessie

I loosen the kung-fu grip I have on my Marketing Principles project report, unraveling it to reread the red *See me* Professor Pfeffer scribbled across the top. I'm missing another dodgeball game to make it to his office hours, a fact that has guilt mingling with anxiety when I picture Team Captain Maddy's disappointed frown.

I knock on the door frame of Professor P.'s office. He looks up at me from a stack of papers and smiles. I take that as a good sign. *He wouldn't be smiling if he's failing me, right?*

"You wanted to see me?" I ask, still hoping there was some sort of mistake. Spending time with Devin, on top of all my other social obligations, hasn't left much time for school. Still, I thought my report on the auto shop was damn good. I've increased their productivity by fifteen percent in the first month, and while business is still picking up, I'm confident in my prediction that within the next six months, new customers will more than make up for the cost of the infrastructure upgrades. But maybe I have no idea what I'm talking about, since I got the college equivalent of being called to the principal's office.

Professor P. waves me in and gestures to the seat in front of his desk. "Yes, please have a seat." He shuffles through open books and folders splayed across his desk. "Where did I put that packet?" he asks one of the stacks.

My knee bounces while I wait for him to tell me what the hell this meeting is about.

"Was there something wrong with my project paper?"

"Wrong?" The shuffling stops and my absent-minded professor looks up at me, confused. "Whatever would give you that idea?"

I hold up the report and point to the three bold exclamation points at the end of his *See me*.

"Oh, that." He waves it away. "No. Your report was unique, ambitious and innovative. You'll receive an A, of course."

Okay, now I'm confused. "Then why —"

"Ah, here it is," he exclaims. "What are your plans after graduation, Ms. Allen?"

My head is spinning and it takes a minute to understand his question, much less find an answer. "Jessie," I say to buy time. "Everyone calls me Jessie."

"Jessie." Professor P. smiles. "What are your plans for the future?"

"Grad school, get an MBA and work for the family business," I utter, like it's my death sentence.

"Hmmm." He ponders my answer. "What would you think about running a state program to revitalize small businesses instead?"

I stare at him, dumbfounded.

"Are you aware I'm the head of a government think tank on economic growth, Ms. Allen?"

"No, I wasn't."

He hands me a thick folder. "I have a pool of funding at my disposal and every year I keep an eye out for promising students with practical ideas. I have to say, your project caught my eye. It is exactly the type of thinking that could help stimulate our state's economy and build a strong small business base."

My mouth drops open. "Your think tank wants to hire me to do more business evaluation?"

"Not quite. I want to give you a grant to work with failing small businesses across the state over the next three to five years to save them from going under." He points to the folder in my hands that I haven't looked at. "That is a grant application package. A formality for the approval, really, but you'd have to provide me with a scope of how many businesses you think you could help in a five-year period along with a set budget for your salary to include travel expenses, any staff or infrastructure you'd need, publicity for the program and, of course, the budget for improvements to each business."

"Holy crap," I swear under my breath.

"Holy crap indeed." Professor P. chuckles.

"Sorry." I flip through the thirty-page grant application, overwhelmed and yet simmering with excitement at the possibilities. "There has to be someone more qualified to do this."

"More qualified on paper perhaps, but I think, to succeed, a project like this needs enthusiasm, optimism and innovation in equal proportions to expertise. It needs someone who looks at failure and sees possibilities. And I think that someone is you, Jessie."

"Wow, thank you so much." I bite my lip, turning the idea over and over in my head. It sounds amazing, getting to work with a new and different business every few months. Finding out what their problem is and fighting to get them to where they need to be. Helping to build something. My heart races with the potential before me. Then my mom's disappointed face flashes in front of me and I let out a long, pained sigh.

Instead of the *yes!* I want to scream, I hear myself asking, "Can I think about it?"

"Of course. I'm looking to make decisions on next year's funding by August, so you have a few months to put together your proposal if you're interested. There's also the possibility of applying some of your efforts and findings towards a work-study MBA program."

"Thank you," I stutter with a nod. In a haze, I stand and stagger out of Professor P.'s office. In my hands is the opportunity of a lifetime. Exciting, challenging and waiting for me. But what do I tell my family? What do I tell Devin?

Too stunned to drive, I take a seat on a bench in the quad and dial Jake's number.

"Jessie Bird, what's up?" my favorite brother asks.

"Was it worth it, Jake?" I sputter without explanation.

"Uhhh, I'm going to need some context to that question to have any hope of answering it. If we're talking about the Louisiana Purchase, that's a hell yeah. If we're talking about the Sonics trading Scottie Pippin, that's a great big fuck no."

"Urgh, you're an idiot."

"You're the one calling me for advice, so…"

"Fine. I'm an idiot too."

Jake chuckles. "Now that we've established we're a family of idiots, was what worth it, sis?"

I take a deep breath and clutch the folder that might hold my future. "Doing your own thing. Was it worth it? All the stress and drama. If you could do it all over again, would you still work for Legal Aid?"

"In a heartbeat," he answers without hesitation.

"But Mom, the guilt…"

"Yeah, I got an earful from Jared and Mom was crushed at first. But in the end, they know I'm doing what I love. And the rest of it doesn't matter. Jessie, Mom wants us to be happy more than anything else. Yeah, she'd be happier if we all lived on some massive Allen family compound with all of us in shouting distance at all times, but *none* of us are going to sign up for that."

I sigh. "There's this thing I might want to do."

"Do it," Jake commands.

"But Mom and Devin are going to lose it — "

"So fucking what? You spend too much time doing what makes everyone else happy and you'll end up miserable, Jessie."

"What if making other people happy makes me happy, smart ass?" I look down at my watch, wondering if I can still make it to the dodgeball game for Maddy.

"You're smarter than that."

"I've gotta go."

"Of course you do." He sighs. "See you next week for dinner?"

"Like I have a choice?" I quip and we both chuckle. "And Jake?"

"Yeah?"

"Thanks."

"Any time, Jessie Bird."

Chapter Twenty-Four

Devin

"Anyone home?" I holler.

"Yeah, coming," Becs calls from her room. I'm taking her out to a movie tonight, one of the traditions we started when she moved in with Rob and Mandy. I wanted to make sure there was still at least one night a week where it was just us, our small two-person family.

I grab a soda out of the fridge and take a sip as I thumb through the mail, waiting on my baby sister to get her butt in gear. A large, fat envelope at the bottom of the stack catches my attention. It's got an Indiana address in the corner and Becs' name on the front. I flip it over and the words *Welcome to Notre Dame!* in green and gold across the back have my blood boiling.

"Ready?" Becs asks, popping into the kitchen without a care in the world.

"What the hell is this?"

Her eyes go wide, but she brushes me off. "Nothing. Just more college stuff."

"Indiana?" I bark out.

She squares her shoulders. "Yes. In Indiana."

"No." She's young. She doesn't know what it's like out there alone. How shitty people can be. And I'm going to do my damnedest to make sure she goes a little bit longer not knowing.

"Notre Dame is one of the best colleges in the country and I've got a full ride." She raises her voice and her hands ball into fists.

"It's dangerous."

"So what? I just shouldn't go to college, then? You want me to work at the shop with you for the rest of my life?" Her words are coated in disgust. Her contempt for my job, my life, is written across her face.

I let out a low sigh. "That's *not* what I'm saying —"

"Oh, better yet, why don't you just lock me here in my room until I die?" she bites out.

This conversation is getting away from me. "There's a college right down the fucking street. You're my baby sister —"

"I am *not* a baby!" Becs shouts at me.

I raise my voice to meet hers. "You sure as shit aren't an adult. You're a stupid kid who thinks running way like her mother did will solve all her problems." The thought of not being there, of someone hurting her, is enough to keep me from being able to see straight. "You're not going all the way to Indiana where I can't protect you. Where I'll never even fucking see you."

"Why do you have to be like this?" I don't answer her rhetorical question. Instead, I stare down at her, arms crossed and jaw set. "Rob and Mandy are fine with me going. Even Jessie wants me to go."

I jab a finger into my chest. "And it doesn't matter what I want? I'm your brother." Your *family*. "All I've

Amelia Kingston

ever wanted to do is *protect* you. How the hell am I supposed to do that two thousand miles away, huh?"

"I don't need protecting!"

"You have no idea the shit that goes down out there. Some guy hurts you, you get scared, what are you going to do?" I stalk toward her, cornering her in the small kitchen.

"I'll handle it." Her voice is fragile, cracking at the edges.

"How?" My hands land on her shoulders, I squeeze hard and try to shake some sense into her. "Show me. Some asshole puts his hands on you, how you going to *handle* it?"

Her breath comes in quick, panicked breaths. She struggles against my grip, pulling away. I don't let her. Frustration and fury make her eyes catch fire. They're brimming with tears when she finally screams, "Devin, let me go!"

I drop my hands and step away. She's sniffing to hold back her sobs, her chest rising and falling in jerky gasps. I scared her. She's never been scared of me before. My heart shatters in my chest. I reach for her.

She slaps away my hand, pulling her shoulders straight. "Don't touch me," she screeches.

"Becs, I'm sor—"

"You're a bully. Just like *him*." Her voice is shaky.

I've broken a piece of her. I see it when her eyes find mine. All I've ever wanted to do is protect her, but I'm the one who hurt her. And I don't know how to fix it. I don't know if I even can.

Chapter Twenty-Five

Jessie

I pull back the sleeves of my unicorn onesie – the official uniform for movie night at the Kappa house – and shove a handful of popcorn into my mouth. I'm curled up on the couch, my phone in my pocket in case Devin decides to learn how to text. I rub the hummingbird pendant around my neck with my non-popcorn hand.

A small part of me feels guilty at not coming clean to Devin for fibbing about losing a necklace, but I'd do it again a million times over if it resulted in the past twenty-four hours. I accidentally told Devin I loved him – it was bound to slip out sooner or later, because the feeling sure as hell isn't going away – and he didn't run. I thought for sure I'd spook the surly giant. It took weeks just to get him to go out with me and another couple of weeks for him to admit he enjoyed it. I thought for sure letting the L-word slip was going to be the end. But it wasn't. Now I just need to find a way to convince him of what our future could be. *If he asks me to stay, will I be able to say no?*

"That's pretty," Megan says, pointing to my new necklace and plopping down next to me in her penguin onesie.

I smile widely. "Birthday present from my boyfriend."

"Awwww," a chorus of my sorority sisters chimes in.

"Seriously? Didn't think you were the boyfriend type," Megan adds.

"What's that supposed to mean?"

"Nothing, you just always seemed to like the chase more than the rest of it."

I tilt my head and think. She's right. With other boys, the game was the fun part. Not with Devin. I sigh, thinking about running my fingers through his hair last night with his head on my chest.

"Guess I was just waiting to let the right one catch me."

"She does exist!" Michelle teases, strutting in from the kitchen in her pink bunny onesie. "The mythical Jessie Bird! More rare than a rainbow unicorn."

"Hardy har har." I toss some popcorn at her and she ducks to catch it in her mouth like some freaky food ninja.

She sweeps behind the couch and wraps her arms around my shoulders. "I've just missed you, babe."

I squeeze her forearm. "I missed you too."

She hops over the couch, embracing her bunny persona, and takes the seat on my other side. "When are we going to meet this hunky boyfriend, anyway?"

"I don't think he's ready for the sisters of Kappa just yet." I laugh. "How are things with Drew?"

Michelle's face drops into a deep frown. "Non-existent. I thought he was a good guy, but turns out he's an asshole like the rest of them. Good riddance." Her voice is detached, but I know her well enough to hear the pain she's concealing underneath.

I open my mouth to ask what happened when Kimmie comes rushing into the living room. Her worried and serious face doesn't match her purple dragon onesie.

"What's wrong, Kimmie?" I stand as she waves me over to the hallway.

"There's a girl here to see you. She seems upset."

I follow her to the front door and find Becs sitting on the bench in our front entrance, her head in her hands and her shoulders shaking with obvious sobs. The sight breaks my heart.

"Oh my gosh, Becs!" Without thinking, I drop to my knees in front of her and wrap her in my arms. She slides to the ground, puts her arms around me and rests her head on my chest like her brother did last night. "Are you okay?" She nods against me, but she's still sobbing and I can't make out her words. "Is Rob —" My stomach flips and I can't finish that sentence. Becs shakes her head again, more violently this time. She takes a deep breath. "Did something happen to Devin?"

"Screw that asshole!" she shouts, and her hazel eyes, red from crying, flash with a ferocious anger. I know that look. Somehow, it's more intimidating coming from petite Becs than burly Devin.

My eyes go wide and my eyebrows shoot into my hairline. "Wow. Okay. Want to tell me what the asshole did?"

"He found out I was accepted to Notre Dame and he lost his mind. He said the only way I'm going to a college out of state is over his dead body."

I tuck a strand of hair behind her ear and rub my hand down her back. "And what did you say?"

"I told him I could make that happen."

Those wild eyes fix on me and I picture this fierce and fiery young woman going toe-to-toe with her overbearing big brother. I lose it. I crack up, letting out a deep laugh and keeling forward until my head hits the floor.

"Make it happen!" I spit out between hysterical fits.

My laughing is contagious and Becs loses it right next to me. I grab my stomach with the ache setting in. We laugh until we're both crying. I take a couple of deep breaths and wipe the tears out of my eyes.

"Oh, I love you, kid."

She smacks me on the shoulder. "I'm not gonna let someone in a unicorn onesie call *me* a kid."

I hold up my hands in submission. "Fair. No need to take me out, killer. Come on, let's get some ice cream and you can tell me all about it." I wrap my arm around her shoulder and lead her into the living room where all my sisters sit, pretending they weren't listening to every word we said.

"Ladies," I announce. "We have an honorary Kappa for the night. This is BB and she needs some serious big sister love. *Stat!*"

My amazing sorority sisters swarm Becs, hovering and cooing as they drag her into the living room and plop her down in the middle of the couch. An ice cream sundae magics its way into her hands, sprinkles and hot fudge included. We don't fuck around with our emotional eating in this house.

Movie night is replaced with Becs' live theater. For an hour, she regales my sisters with tales of Devin, the overbearing asshole. I don't correct her or try to defend him, even when she makes him sound worse than any evil villain ever created. Right now, it's clear she needs to vent and feel supported without judgment. I bet that's why she came to me instead of Rob and Mandy.

I know Devin loves her more than anything, and while he may be a dick sometimes—okay, most of the time—he would do anything to keep her safe...including make her miserable. When she's calmed down and eaten her body weight in ice cream, I'll try to explain that to her.

My phone rings in my fuzzy pocket and every eye in the room shoots to me with judgment, like we were in a dark movie theater instead of my noisy living room. I pull it out and bite my lip when I see Devin's name flashing across the screen.

I hold it up to all the girls. "Speak of the asshole."

Becs' face scrunches up like she just bit into a lemon.

"Did you tell him where you were going?" I ask her.

She shakes her head. "I just stormed out and slammed the door behind me," she snips with her nose in the air.

"You go, girl!" Michelle cheers from the corner of the couch.

Not helpful, Michelle.

"He's not my dad. It's none of his business where I am."

I step toward the kitchen. "I'm going to answer it real quick."

A collective gasp sucks the air out of the room. *Jesus, sorority girls can be so damn dramatic.*

I weigh my words carefully, making sure I don't become public enemy number one. "I'm just going to tell him you're safe. I'm sure he's worried."

Becs crosses her arms and scowls at me. Damn, she is so much like her brother. I'm careful to keep the smile off my lips.

"If I don't answer, you know he's just going to come over and bust the door down to make sure you're okay."

"Fine," Becs sighs with an eye-roll.

I dart into the kitchen, but the call has already gone to voicemail. I click over and listen real quick.

"Jessie. Devin. Had a fight with Becs. She ran out. I can't find her. Call me."

The message is short and direct. Very Devin. It's not the words he says but his voice that turns my stomach. It's a mix of desperation, anger and regret. My fingers fly across the keys, eager to take away his pain.

"Jessie—" His voice is ragged and exhausted.

"She's here. She's fine. Safe," I spit out.

He lets out a deep breath, one I bet he's been holding since she slammed the door in his face. "I'm coming over."

"That's not a good idea."

"I'm coming over," he repeats, the tension in his voice palpable over the roar of his engine in the background.

"Devin—" I don't get a chance to talk him out of it because the line goes dead. *The asshole hung up on me.* Okay. Now I'm pissed too.

And that's how I ended up sitting alone on my front porch in my stupid onesie, the clink of moths crashing into the porchlight above my head the only distraction from the cold. My movie night has gone up in flames thanks to Bennett family drama. I hear Devin's car barreling down the dark street before I can see it. The slam of his car door tells me the drive hasn't chilled him out one bit.

"Where is she?" he barks, marching up the driveway.

Hello to you too. My night's going great, thanks for asking.

I stand up, brushing the dirt off my butt flap. "Inside, being doted on by my entire sorority. Other than gaining a few extra pounds, she's perfectly safe."

"She's coming home." Devin grabs the doorknob, but I slam a hand into his chest to get the monster's attention.

"No. She's not. Like I said on the phone, you coming over was *not* a good idea." He growls at me, not stepping back. I hold my ground, my eyes locked on his to let him know he doesn't scare me. I know this beast sleeps in a giant heap of pillows, puts half a bag of sugar in his coffee and loves to cuddle more than anything. He's not intimidating anyone on this porch.

He leans forward, putting pressure on my hand in his chest, but my arm doesn't buckle.

"She took off because you were being an overbearing jerk. Take it from a girl with three brothers, you go in there now with this attitude and you'll only make it worse. She'll rabbit on you again. And next time, she'll go somewhere you aren't going to find her so easily."

He shakes his head and steps back.

"Not to mention, my sisters might murder you before you get to her. She's become a bit of a Kappa house mascot."

He lets out a quick hum. Not quite a laugh, but almost. He runs his hands through his dark hair and those coal-black eyes take me in.

"What the hell are you wearing?"

I smile and wiggle my eyebrows. "This old thing? You like?"

He shakes his head and lets out a full laugh this time. He's quiet for a bit, staring off into the night. "How bad is it?" he asks, a deep frown on his face.

I let out a long breath, letting it whistle through my lips. "Pretty bad. She was bawling her eyes out when she showed up."

"*Fuck*," he curses himself under his breath.

I plop down onto the stoop and tap the spot next to me. "Pull up some porch, Big Man."

He eases his hulking frame down next to me, his legs wide, brushing against mine.

"So, wha'chya do?" I ask, keeping my voice light.

He lets out a long sigh and slumps forward, like the weight of the world is crushing him. "I fucked up, JB. I said some shit I shouldn't've. Then she took off and I lost my fucking mind. I can't lose her too."

I slide my hand into his, resting my chin on his shoulder and keeping quiet. He looks at my hand in his.

"When Becs was born, she was so small. Her little hand barely fit around my finger." Devin sandwiches my hand with his, flipping it over and over and studying it like I'm another species. "She was a preemie. Two months early." His expression goes blank and his eyes are vacant. He's staring off into the night when he begins again. "I tried to make sure my dad didn't touch my mom while she was pregnant. Took enough beatings for the both of us. But one night, he came home after a poker game. Broke. Drunk. And pissed. I shoved him as soon as he walked in the door, picking a fight. He beat me almost unconscious. Mom tried to pull him off, scared he'd kill me. He tossed her against the wall and her water broke." His voice is cold and flat. "I was eight."

My chest breaks wide open for him. For his mother. For an unborn baby Bennett. Tears sting my eyes. I grab his hands with both of mine, our twenty fingers curling together in a human puzzle. I don't say anything. There's no apology big enough for what he's been through.

"Becs doesn't know she was born on our living room floor, surrounded by paramedics right after our dad got carted off to jail. She doesn't know how bad it was. How hard I tried to keep the three of us together. How scared I am that part of him is in me."

I grab his chin and turn him to face me. I shake my head as tears trail down my face. "You are *not* him. You'd never let anyone hurt her."

"*I* hurt her!" he snarls, ripping his hands out of mine. "I told her she's stupid and selfish like our mother. I scared her." He drops his head into his hands and sobs. He looks just like his baby sister did a few hours ago. Broken. "And she told me I was just like *him*."

I run my fingers through his hair and squeeze his knee, desperate to provide any comfort I can. "She didn't mean it. You didn't mean it. You were both hurt and upset."

He lifts his head and gazes into me. His eyes are black holes, liquid darkness swirling with years of pain. "What if she's right? What if I hurt people, like him?"

"You're not. I see you." I lean into him, sealing my mouth on his and pouring my love into him. Against his lips I whisper, "You think you're tough, making people scale those walls you've built. Barbed wire and all. But, behind it, you're the most loving man I've ever met."

He lets out a ragged breath. "I don't blame my mom for taking off. Or for not taking me with her. I look just like him. Don't think she ever really trusted me 'cause of that." He chokes on the held-back tears. "But she should've taken the baby. Becs deserves better than me."

"You *both* deserved better." I pepper his face with soft, slow kisses.

He pulls me into his lap, wrapping me in his arms and burying his face in my neck. He takes slow, deep breaths, squeezing me to him. I hug him in turn, trying to convince him he's everything a man should be.

* * * *

I have an emotional hangover from last night. Between finding Becs sobbing and Devin's confession about his past, my heart is still recovering. A girl can only take so much.

My first class isn't until ten this morning, so I have plenty of time to sip my coffee and think of the best strategy for talking to Becs. I understand why she's upset. With three bossy brothers looking over my shoulder, I know *exactly* how she feels. She just wants to stretch her wings and Devin's keeping her shackled to the ground. He thinks telling her how dangerous it is to fly will keep her from wanting to feel the wind on her face.

Not gonna happen, bud.

I know he just wants to keep her close. Keep her safe. He's lost everything and losing her too might just destroy him. But the harder he fights to keep her, the more she'll want to get away. I can see both sides, but I hate being in the middle. Someone's got to keep the peace, and since I love the hell out of both of them, I guess today that someone is me.

"Rise and shine, lioness." I pull back the hood on the lion onesie Michelle let Becs borrow last night, and the lump of blankets starts to move. And groan.

"Five more minutes," she whines.

I tug off the rest of the blankets. "Not happening, sister." I slap her on the butt and she sits upright. "How you feeling this morning?"

She takes the coffee. "Pissed. And tired."

I hum in acknowledgment. "So, what's the plan?"

"I don't know. I want Notre Dame so bad. But the way Devin reacted last night…" She sighs, her shoulders sagging. "He's going to make me choose. Him or my dream school."

I sink down into the couch next to her, propping my elbow on the back and resting my head on it. "I think he reacted so bad because he *found out* instead of you *telling* him about it. He kinda hates being the last to know. Trust me."

Becs nods. "Yeah, I guess that didn't help. But, seriously, do you think my brother will *ever* let me get farther than arm's reach?"

"Give him some time. Let him get used to the idea." I don't hide my uncertainty. Devin hates change and he's terrified of losing the people he loves. Becs leaving is pretty much his worst nightmare. *Guess I shouldn't tell him about the grant any time soon.*

"I should just go. Wake up one morning and be gone. The jerk deserves that," Becs snaps.

I shake my head and give her a stern look. "No, he doesn't. And you know it."

"He's smothering me. He's not my dad," she whines. I bite my tongue. Devin's been more of a father than a brother her whole life, and now I know why.

"He's not, but he loves you. And you're the only real family he has."

"For now, maybe."

"What's that supposed to mean?"

"That maybe if you gave him a couple babies of his own to worry about, he'd get off my case."

I let out a nervous laugh. "My womb is not your golden parachute, BB."

"Fine. It'd take too long to get you knocked up anyway. If I miss Freshman orientation next week, I forfeit my spot."

Jake's words filter back into my mind. *'Spend too much time doing what makes everyone else happy and you'll end up miserable.'* Devin isn't ready to let her go yet, but it will destroy him to know he kept her from her dream.

"Then go," I declare. "It's just a weekend, right? And it'll keep your options open until you can have an adult conversation with Devin."

Her eyes go wide. "Are you kidding? He went berserk, nearly calling the cops when I stormed out of the house for a few hours! Can you imagine what would happen if I left for a *whole weekend*? He'd drive to Indiana and drag me back kicking and screaming."

"What do Rob and Mandy have to say?" I ask, wondering for the millionth time why her parents aren't the ones having this conversation with her. And with Devin.

She groans. "Nothing. They're sweet and supportive and tell me I can be anything I want. But what does that matter if I leave and my giant butthead of a big brother never wants to speak to me again?"

I reach out and squeeze her knee. "He's pissed, but I think he's hurt and scared more than anything. He's not going to cut you out of his life, you have to know that."

She looks down at her hands and her eyes get watery. "I don't know, Jessie. Some of the things he said last night…"

"You guys both said some stuff you didn't mean."

She nods, swallowing to hold back the tears.

"You're going to Notre Dame and Devin's going to be okay with it," I tell her, my voice light and enthusiastic.

Becs stares at me like I suggested we climb Mount Everest butt naked.

"I'm dead serious. We can make this happen. Apply a little time and a bit of pressure and that brother of yours cracks open like a cheap piggy bank. Trust me." I give her a wicked grin.

"Pressure I'm fine with. But I don't have time. Freshman orientation is *next* weekend." She deflates.

"Then I'll go for you."

"What?" She pops up, spilling her now lukewarm coffee over the front of Michelle's lion onesie.

"You just need someone to show up and sign your name, right?" She nods vigorously, spilling more coffee. I pry it out of her hands and stare at those big, pleading eyes. "Then I'll go for you. You'll keep your spot and we'll work on warming Devin up to the idea."

"You'd do that for me?" Her lip quivers.

"Anything for you, BB."

She shoots across the couch and tackles me in a bear hug, spilling my coffee this time.

"Thankyouthankyouthankyou," she says all in one breath. "You know Devin's going to be pissed at you for this, right?"

I wince. "Maybe we wait to tell him until he's had time to adjust to the idea of you going away to school."

"He likes secrets about as much as he likes change."

I'm not comfortable with hiding something like this from Devin, but I don't see any other option right now. Trust doesn't come easy for him and helping his baby sister leave the state would pretty much be the ultimate betrayal. Add to it that I'm thinking of taking a job that would require me to travel across the state for the next five years and I'm pretty sure he'd never forgive me. I just need to buy a little more time.

"Well, guess we better make sure he doesn't find out, then."

Chapter Twenty-Six

Devin

Jessie sends me a text to let me know she's back. She's been distant and cryptic for the past week, telling me she was going to be out of town for a few days but never saying where or why. I could ask, but I'm pissed I have to. My girlfriend still doesn't seem to want to tell me what's going on in her life. After finding out what a piece of shit my father is, the kind of things I'm capable of, I'm not surprised she's been distant. Who'd want to be with someone who's got a devil scratching to get out of them?

Pissed or not, I finish up at work and head straight to her place. I need her help, her advice on how to fix this shit with Becs. But I also need to see her sweet smile. Hold her soft curves against me. I need to know she's still here. *Still mine.*

She opens her front door with a surprised, happy look on her face. Those green eyes sparkle even brighter than I remember. She squeals with joy, wrapping her arms around my neck and her legs around my waist. I chuckle, burying my face in her neck and breathing in her sweet vanilla smell. I let out a heavy sigh, my body relaxing for the first time in days.

"Hi," she whispers in my ear.

"Hey," I mumble back.

She hops down, grabs my hand and drags me up to her room. The door closes and I'm on her, pressing our bodies together and stealing kisses. A warm hum rumbles in her chest.

I drop my forehead to hers. "I missed you."

She giggles, tips up on her toes and plants a chaste kiss on my lips. "I can tell." She turns and struts over to the bed, leveling me with the naughty look in her eye.

"Come here, Big Man."

I slide over to her desk, keeping my eyes locked on her as she lies down on the bed. My dick aches to be between those long legs. Without looking, I open the drawer where she keeps her condoms and rifle around, but come up empty. Finally tearing my eyes off her, I look down and realize I opened the wrong drawer. Instead of condoms, I'm staring down into a stack of letters. My brain can't make sense of what I'm seeing, but the sinking feeling in the pit of my stomach grows when I pick up the pile.

"Devin…" Jessie's voice sounds distant as it echoes in the back of my mind.

I thumb through the papers, reading the names and addresses on the fancy letterhead. Graduate school acceptance letters. Graduate schools *out of state*. We've never talked about it, but I assumed she was staying here. Her family is here. Her friends are here. *I'm here*. She'd tell me if she was leaving.

"What is this?" I ask, blindsided.

"It's not what it looks like." She scrambles off the bed, her hands held up in surrender and a guilty look on her face.

"Then what is it?" My voice is sharp when I slap the letters down on her desk.

"They're just acceptance letters, that's all." She swallows and bites her lip, looking guilty as shit when she adds, "But there's something I've been meaning to talk to you about. I have an opportunity —"

I shake my head. "Opportunity," I repeat her word, rolling it over and over in my head. *Escape*. That's what she means. Escaping this town. This life. *Me*.

In the middle of Jessie breaking my heart, my baby sister comes bounding in with one of Jessie's sorority sisters hot on her heels. "Jessie? How was it? Did you love the campus? Tell me *everything*." My sister's singsong voice fills the small bedroom.

"Becs," Jessie shouts out a quick warning, shaking her head. Becs and the other girl stop dead in their tracks. Becs' eyes go wide and she gasps in shock at seeing me standing in my girlfriend's room.

"No, JB. Tell us. I want to know. How was the campus?" I spit venom, glaring at her with sheer loathing in my eyes.

"Devin..." Jessie's voice is a soft warning.

I snatch up the pile of acceptance letters. "Which one was it? Northwestern?" I toss the letter in the air, moving on to the next. "Michigan? North Carolina?" I glare at Becs frozen in the doorway. "Indiana?" I toss the rest of the letters at Jessie's feet. "That's where you went this weekend, isn't it? To look at some school a thousand miles away." My heart is surging in my chest, ripping itself apart with the need to hear her tell me it's not true. She's not going anywhere. She's staying here. *Staying mine.*

"Yes. I went to look at a school out of state," Jessie answers flatly, her back straight and her eyes clear.

"Devin, it's my fau—" Becs starts, tears in her eyes as she glances back and forth between Jessie and me.

"Becs, this has *nothing* to do with you," Jessie cuts her off. "This is about your brother not trusting me." Jessie and I square off, eyes locked, wills warring. "I thought we could have a calm and rational adult conversation about our future, but I guess I was wrong."

The air has been sucked out of the room and I'm suffocating.

"What future? You're leaving." I look over at Becs. "You're both fucking leaving."

"That's what you think? That we don't have a future?" Jessie's eyes narrow and her nostrils flare.

"You leaving?" I answer her question with a question.

"It's complicated."

I shake my head and glare at her. "No. It's not."

Feet shuffle by the door and in my peripheral vision I see the girl I don't know put a hand on Becs' shoulders before she says, "We should go."

"No," I snarl. "I'll leave. It's my turn, isn't it?" I cross the room to Jessie, stepping into her until our chests collide. She holds my gaze, strong as steel. I lean down to her, brushing the pendant around her neck with the pad of my thumb, and whisper, "You've got your freedom now, little hummingbird. Fly away. See if I care."

Her face is unmoved, sneer locked in place. The only signs she heard me at all are the few quick blinks of those beautiful green eyes that are shining with tears.

Chapter Twenty-Seven

Jessie

My heart races with rage and frustration. The moment I see Devin's back disappear through my bedroom door, I let out an exasperated roar.

"What an asshole!" If he's still in the house, he must've heard me. A fire blazes in my chest and I collapse onto the bed, gasping for breath. My shoulders tremble with the mix of fury and heartbreak.

Becs and Michelle rush over, each taking a seat beside me. They wrap their arms around me and speak soothing words into my ears, but I can't hear any of it. Devin's gone. He walked out like it was nothing. Like I meant nothing. I didn't even get the chance to tell him about the grant, to ask him to come with me. One misunderstanding was all it took for him to give up on me. On us.

"It'll be okay, JB," Michelle promises. The sound of my nickname twists the knife Devin plunged into my heart and the tears start in earnest. The sobs bubble up from somewhere deep in my chest. A dam has broken loose and I can't stem the tide of sorrow washing over me. I keel forward, my head dropping in my hands as my tears drop to the floor.

The three of us sit in the quiet. Our roles now reversed, Becs rubs my back in slow, soothing circles. She is choked with guilt when she says, "I'll tell him the truth. He's already pissed at me anyway."

"No," I snap. "He can't pretend he loves me but not trust me. How could he think I'm planning on leaving?"

"Well, weren't you?" Michelle asks, leaning down to pick up the scattered, offending letters.

I glare at her. "Not like that. Not anymore. Not without him."

"Then why didn't you tell him?"

"I don't know!" I sobbed. They watch me pace with concern and confusion etched in their faces. *Because I was afraid he'd say no.*

"You weren't really going to leave, were you?" Becs asks, her voice betraying her own distrust.

I shake my head, my eyebrows pinching together in annoyance. "No. Yes. Maybe."

Becs snatches the papers and waves them in front of me in silent accusation. I rip them out of her hands, toss them back in the drawer they came from and slam it shut with an echoing thud. "I thought maybe he'd come with me. Or, I don't know. I've been offered this amazing grant—"

"Wow," Becs scoffs and Michelle audibly winces.

I level the kid with one of her brother's devastating scowls. "Ever heard the one about the pot and the kettle, BB?"

She jumps up off the bed and squares off with me. "Hey, don't turn this around on me. That's different."

"Oh, right!"

"It is." Her voice rises and our eyes lock. Michelle sits on the edge of the bed, riveted, her gaze darting between Becs and me like we're the final match at Wimbledon. "I *know* what I want. The *one* thing I want. Notre Dame. I'm not talking about other *opportunities* and stringing along my brother for fun. He wants to start a life with you, Jessie."

"I know." I shriek. I rip open the drawer, pull out the letters and tear them into tiny shreds until they match my tattered heart. I toss the pieces in the air and they rain down on us like confetti. I peer at Becs through the paper storm. "I love him, Rebecca Bennett."

Becs takes in the mess surrounding us with a satisfied smirk. "Okay then."

"Go get him," Michelle adds, beaming like she's watching some Hallmark movie.

I stare at the ground. "No."

"Why not?" Michelle and Becs ask in unison.

"Because I'm willing to give up everything." I gesture to the shreds of my future littering the floor then to the door. "And *he* walked out on me like it was nothing. Like what we have doesn't matter."

"He's just hurt." Michelle squeezes my arm.

"You know how he loves surprises," Becs deadpans.

"I'm sure he'll calm down," Michelle adds.

"I don't care if he wants me again when he calms down. The point is he walked away. He *can* walk away." I flop down on my bed. "I've been chasing him since day one. Pushing. Prodding. Blackmailing. I made this happen. He's just been along for the ride." I pull my shoulders back and stare straight ahead. "Well, the ride's over. I'm done chasing after Devin Bennett."

* * * *

I throw myself into every activity I can find. There's not a spare second in my day to think about Devin. Except I still do. All day. Every day. In class. At volleyball. During study group. While I'm writing my grant proposal for Professor P. Sitting at the table during dinner with my family. I obsess over every touch, every kiss, every word. I miss him. I miss his smell and his scowl. I miss his smile and his groan. I miss the mix of tender harshness.

I kept the promise I made to myself the day he stormed out. I haven't called him. I haven't gone by the shop. I haven't asked Becs about him. I'm giving him the distance he's always wanted and it's killing me. I feel like a Jenga tower with half the pieces missing, shaky and incomplete. A strong breeze and I'll topple to the ground.

Despite the few nights I convinced myself I saw his car driving by my house, I haven't heard from Devin in two weeks. Becs texts me every day. Nothing that matters, just small stupid jokes and memes, like she's scared I'll fade away if she doesn't keep reaching out. I might. I love Becs. I love Rob and Mandy. I love that stupid repair shop and all the crazy people in it. But for now, at least, they're too painful to be around. My phone buzzes in my pocket with a text from Becs.

Come by the shop at five today. I've got something to tell you. Don't worry, he-who-shall-not-be-named won't be here.

Electricity shoots across my body at the idea of returning to the shop. The chance of seeing Devin again makes my mind race and my heart do backflips. I don't answer and she texts again.

Everyone misses you! Rob keeps sniffling when he looks at your computer system. He says it's allergies, but I'm not buying it.

Becs has no qualms about playing dirty. She knows I adore that man and his bushy mustache. I text back that I'll try, not wanting to confirm for sure where I'll be or when, just in case this is a set-up.

I drive through the parking lot slowly, checking each and every car to make sure Devin's isn't here. My stomach is churning and my heart is racing. I feel like I'm slipping behind enemy lines. The familiar bell over the door announces my arrival. Rob and Becs, who were both engrossed with a magazine on the counter, look up to find me standing in the shop, waving awkwardly.

"Jessie!" Becs squeals, jumping over the counter and rushing at me. She wraps her arms around me, tighter than a boa constrictor. Rob's warm chuckle soothes my nerves as he hugs the both of us.

"We missed you around here. This one most of all," Rob tells me. Becs levels him with a stern gaze. "Well, second most, I suppose." My heart swirls in my chest at the off-hand comment. He must be talking about Devin. *Has he missed me?* I can't picture it. He's too mad at me to miss me.

I avoid the bait and slip out of the group hug. "I missed *you two* too." I slink over to the far side of the shop, peeking into the office to make sure he's not lurking in the back.

"He's not here." Becs' voice startles me as I search the small office with my eyes, picturing every inch of Devin's large body from memory.

I clear my throat and force lightness into my voice. "Okay. So, what's this news you had to tell me in person?"

Becs bounces over to the magazine on the counter. I follow behind her, still nervous and on edge, scanning the small shop for the man I love and am desperate to avoid.

"I'm going!" Becs declares in victory. I shake my head, trying to focus on my friend. Seeing that I'm not following, she holds up the magazine. Not a magazine, a brochure. *For Notre Dame.* "I'm going to Notre Dame."

I hug her tight. "That's great, Becs. I'm so happy for you." I try to find the words to ask about Devin, but can't.

"We had a family meeting." She looks over at Rob, gratitude carved into her delicate features. "Rob and Mandy are going to drive me there in the fall and stay for a little while to help me get settled."

My eyebrows knit together and I stare at Rob, the peacemaker. *How did he get Devin to agree to this?*

"It's hard to let go of your baby, but that's what being a parent is. You do it right, and someday your little bird's going to leave the nest." Rob wraps an arm around Becs' shoulders with a proud grin. "But seeing 'em soar helps soothes the pain of not being needed."

We all know he's talking about Devin. He must've accepted that, no matter how tightly he held on, at some point Becs is going to grow up. She isn't going to need him forever.

"I still need you guys!" Becs answers. "Who else is going to do my laundry?"

We share a light laugh until the sound of the shop bell sends a jolt of electricity down my spine. I keep my eyes on Becs and Rob, refusing to turn to see who's joined our little party. The way Becs' eyes go wide and Rob begins fussing with the computer tells me who it is. I take a deep breath and hold it, willing my heart to slow down and my stomach to settle. My skin prickles with terrified excitement.

"You said you were going to be gone for two hours," Becs accuses.

"Sorry to disappoint," Devin growls back.

I shut my eyes against the onslaught of emotion. Hearing his deep voice tears me apart. Becs grabs my hand behind the counter, where Devin can't see, and gives an apologetic squeeze.

Wiping the pain off my face, I turn to look at him. Despite my best efforts to steel myself, I gasp at the sight. His broad shoulders, his strong arms, his trim waist. His judgmental scowl. He is a beautiful devil, existing only to torture me.

"Devin," I call his name in a quick, detached greeting. An immobile statue, he doesn't so much as nod.

"I'd better get going," I tell Becs and Rob. I give them both a quick hug before I flit across the shop, moving as quick as I can without seeming like I'm running away. Devin's still standing by the door, refusing to move. It's impossible to leave without brushing past him, and the familiar scent of citrus and machinery makes my knees weak. I grip the door and step into the sun. I'm desperate for the safety of my car, debating sprinting across the parking lot, when I hear the sound of Devin's boots following behind me. He reaches out and grabs my arm, taking a deep breath and holding me in place.

"That's it?" he asks in a harsh whisper.

My pulse is pounding in my ears. The sun is beating down on my flushed face while Devin's fingers burn into the skin on my arm.

"What else is there?" I ask, happy my voice doesn't betray the terror coursing through my body.

His grip relaxes and he traces down my arm with his fingers until his palm finds mine. He squeezes but says nothing. We stare at our clasped hands, both afraid to let go.

"I owe you an apology," I start, unsure if anything I say will matter. "You were right. I'm leaving. I should've told you. I was trying to find a way, but after everything that happened with Becs, I just didn't know how." I close my eyes and force away the tears. I swallow the sadness and push on. "I was afraid. That you'd say no. Or that you'd ask me to choose. That I might lose you." I let out a tortured laugh. "Guess it doesn't matter now. I lost you anyway."

I force myself to meet his eyes. I need to know he hears me. "I'm starting a program to help small businesses. For the next few years, I'll be traveling around the state, doing what we did here." I nod behind him to the shop. "It's what I want to do."

He lets go of my hand and a twinge of sadness flashes across his stoic face. Most people would miss it, but I know him too well and I'm looking too hard not to see. I close my eyes and let my head drop back, the hot sun on my face no match for the fire burning in my heart for this man.

Tears choke my voice when I confess, "I wish I was stronger, but I'm not." I shake my head and stare into those beautiful coal black eyes. "I can't be with you like this. Halfway. I love you too much. I'd make myself miserable trying to make you happy."

I force myself to walk away, my heart breaking in my chest with every step. I refuse to let myself look back.

Chapter Twenty-Eight

Devin

My pointless alarm goes off at six and my fist comes down with a vengeance on the Snooze button. I didn't fall asleep last night. I haven't slept for shit in the weeks since I walked out of Jessie's bedroom. I thought walking away would be easier than getting strung along, but I can still smell her on my pillows. I hear her laugh in the silence. I see her everywhere, catching imagined glimpses of her wherever I go. It's worst in the shop. That place is my second home, but these days it tortures me with memories of the crazy woman who stomped on my heart.

Her words from yesterday have been ringing in my ears ever since. *Halfway.* Is that what she thinks I'm doing with her? I wanted to scream at her. *She's* the one only halfway in. She's got one foot here with me and one foot in some other future. So, I let her go. Or, at least I'm trying to.

My alarm blares on my nightstand again and I send it sailing across the room. I take one last breath of Jessie's sweet smell on my pillow before I strip the bed, tossing the sheets into the hamper with a twinge of regret.

I make it to the shop and dive into work. I haven't had the patience to work behind the counter this week, so I'm out in the bays, ripping an engine apart while Rob deals with our customers. I glare at him through the glass. I don't know what him and Becs were trying to do yesterday, having Jessie show up here just to torture me, but I'm pissed about it. This is my shop. My space. I don't need her here. I've got enough memories to make me miserable for a lifetime. My mind flashes back to giving Jessie her necklace. Of taking her on the hood of a car in this bay. I toss aside my wrench and stalk into the shop.

"What the hell was that yesterday?" I bark at Rob.

Rob's mustache twitches, an easy tell that he's annoyed. Still, he keeps his voice calm. "Your sister wanted to see her friend. Do you have a problem with that?"

"When that friend is my ex and she's in my shop, yes. I do." I cross my arms and scowl at him.

"What are you playing at, son?" Rob asks on a long sigh. I don't answer. "You're in love with that girl. That much is plain as day."

I don't deny it. "And?"

"And, if you don't mind me sayin' so, you're going about it back ass-wards." His tone is the same I use to tell a hipster his ancient Saab is beyond saving. It leaves no room for doubt or argument.

"I mind."

Rob watches me with detached curiosity.

I run my fingers through my hair and take a few breaths. "She's planning on leaving and she has the balls to tell me I'm only in this *halfway*."

Rob rubs his mustache like it's the source of all his worldly wisdom. "She tell you she's leaving?"

I nod. "Eventually."

"She ask you to go with her?"

I shake my head.

"Would you if she did?"

"What the fuck does that matter?" We both know the answer. I would. If she asked me to, I'd go to the moon and back for that woman.

Rob hums. "You scared of losing her?"

"Already lost her," I snap.

Rob shakes his head. "Nah. Jessie loves you. She's just scared too."

"She's got no reason to be scared. I'm *here*," I snarl, slapping my chest.

Rob looks me up and down. "You tell her that? You tell her you love her? That you're willing to go wherever she's going?"

I pull my shoulders straight and glare at him. "Don't have to tell her. I've *shown* her."

Rob glares right back. "Yeah? What've you done to show that woman you're all in?"

I rack my brain for an answer, but can't think of one. She *must* know.

"You can be brave and show her. Or, you can keep bein' stupid and let her go."

Could it be that simple?

Rob crosses the shop, slapping a hand on my shoulder. "Either way, stop bein' such an asshole. You're scaring away all our new customers."

I know she's worth it. Worth chasing to the ends of the earth. But I've never gotten off my selfish, stubborn ass to bother showing her what she means to me.

"I need to take a few days off," I tell Rob.

He nods. "Good. Bring that girl home. Mandy's ready for grandbabies."

I shake my head, ignoring Rob's comment and the smile it put on my lips. I grab my phone out of my pocket and call Austin as I slide in behind the wheel of my car.

"What's up, Dev?" Austin asks.

"Need your help, man." I grip the steering wheel, hating what I know I've got to do. "Elizabeth with you?"

"Yeah, whaddya need?"

I tell him what I've got in mind, and after a solid five minutes of laughing at my expense, he's ready to make shit happen.

If Jessie doesn't know what I'm willing to do to keep her, she sure as fuck will soon. I just hope to hell it works.

Chapter Twenty-Nine

Jessie

In a weird role reversal, nerdy and conservative Elizabeth is digging through my closet on Friday night looking for a cute outfit for me to wear. She's been relentless for the past forty-eight hours, begging me to come out with her to celebrate the end of the term. I said no the first two hundred times she asked. I've ditched out on every single social obligation for the past week. 'No' is my new favorite word.

Seeing Devin again, telling him it was over and not having him fight it, has left me listless and exhausted. My sorority sisters have taken turns feeding me, bringing me mac and cheese, pancakes or ice cream on the days I couldn't be bothered to get out of bed.

"Go shower. Your stink is starting to reach the hallways," Michelle teases. She's joking, I think. I showered yesterday. *Didn't I?*

"Fine." I sulk on my way to the shower. I turn the water up as hot as I can stand it, eager to feel much of anything.

Michelle does my makeup and Elizabeth combs through my hair, pinning it in a cute but messy updo. "This is exactly what you need. A girls' night!" Michelle giggles. "We're going to find you someone even *hotter* than Devin tonight!"

Elizabeth clears her throat and squeezes my shoulders. "If you're ready…"

I blink away the tears. "I'm not."

"Okay," Elizabeth's voice is warm and soothing in my ear. She's had her heart broken. She knows how much I'm hurting right now.

"Well, then just enjoy torturing all those guys in this dress," Michelle muses, applying lip gloss to my pout. "I'm going through a penis-free phase too. Let them eat their egotistical, idiotic, unreliable hearts out."

I'm a mute passenger along for the ride, not paying attention to where the Uber is taking us until we're already standing in the parking lot. I stare up at the bar's neon sign and my stomach twists like a pit of angry snakes.

"Not here. I can't," I plead with Elizabeth, shaking my head hard enough that some of my hair escapes the pinned mess on my head.

"It looks a little rough, Lizbit," Michelle says next to me. It's not the dive bar I object to. It's the fact that it's Devin's dive bar that I have a problem with.

"I swear, it's not as shady as it looks. It'll be fun. They have karaoke tonight!" Elizabeth sings.

"This is where Devin and I had our first date," I confess.

Elizabeth's kind eyes go wide. "I didn't know. I'm sorry. Austin didn't say…" Her voice trails off and she pulls her phone out of her purse. "I'll grab another Uber and we'll go somewhere else." She stares at her phone, biting her lip in concentration. Regret fills her eyes and guilt twists her lips. "The closest one is over twenty minutes away." She blows out a defeated sigh.

"Should we go grab a drink while we wait?" Michelle asks. I balk, not wanting to go inside. "I'm sure Devin's not here."

I wince at the sound of his name. I look over to Elizabeth, silently pleading with her to wait outside with me.

"One drink?" she asks.

I check my watch, then look up and down the dark street. There isn't anywhere else to wait. I glue a fake grin on my face. "Sure. Why not?"

Michelle wraps her arm around mine, doing the same with Elizabeth on the other side, and the three of us stroll into the dive bar like a pack on the prowl. I'm thankful for Michelle's support at my side when my knees buckle at the memories rushing over me. Devin and me, hiding in a dark corner, kissing and touching. *Falling in love.*

"I need a drink." I dash to the bar, flagging down the bartender. "Tequila," I call out as soon as he makes eye contact. He pours me a shot. I down it without a chaser, gesturing for another.

"Wow," Michelle snickers.

Elizabeth sets a hand on my forearm, keeping me from taking my second shot. "Are you okay?"

I nod a half dozen times and chuckle like a lunatic. "Yep. Just dandy," I answer, shooting back the tequila. I clap my hands together, hard enough to sting my palms. The sound is loud and draws attention even in the rowdy bar.

Elizabeth is furiously typing on her phone, no doubt urging our Uber driver to risk life and limb speeding to get here sooner. Michelle is oblivious to my suffering. "Let's dance!" she sings.

"Sure. Why the fuck not?" I answer, my derision coated in sweetness.

The three of us gyrate on the dance floor, Michelle having fun, me faking it and Elizabeth looking between us with a worried mother-hen expression. I grab her hands and twist her back and forth, forcing her to dance. "It's fine. Really. You didn't know."

She bites her lip and glances up at the stage with guilty eyes. The music dies out and the place goes quiet. Everyone turns to the stage. I don't believe it.

This can't be happening.

Devin can't be standing on that stage, staring down at me. I squeeze my eyes closed, willing away the dream. The waking nightmare.

I peel them open, but he's still standing there, looking as beautiful as ever. He's tall, dark and tortured. I can't look away. My masochistic heart soars at the sight, aching to be near him, no matter how much it hurts. At my side, Elizabeth mutters about how sorry she is. She doesn't matter. Michelle doesn't matter. All I can see is Devin, standing on stage with his eyes burning through me.

I take in a sharp breath when he steps up to the microphone and his delicious voice bellows, "This song is for Jessica Allen. I love you, JB. And I'm all in."

My mouth drops open and tears prick my eyes as Devin begins to sing Nirvana's *All Apologies* with sweet soulfulness. He hates talking and loathes singing. I can't imagine anything Devin Bennett would hate more than being on that stage right now in front of a bunch of rowdy drunks. And yet, he closes his eyes and commits to each and every lyric, singing his apology to me. For me.

I listen to his deep and tender song, gravitating towards the stage. Leave it to Devin to use his actions instead of his words. His apology isn't a rehearsed speech about how much I mean to him or a blurted-out confession of his deepest feelings. He's showing me what he'll do to make me happy, to keep me. And it's enough. It's everything. Tears are streaming down my face when he stops. He opens his eyes again, searching for me. They flash with panic when he doesn't find me where I used to be standing.

I smile up at him from the edge of the stage. "Down here, Big Man."

Relief washes over his features and he jumps off the stage, sweeping me into his arms. The room erupts in applause and I can't help but let out a self-conscious laugh. Devin doesn't bother looking up or acknowledging his fans. He's cupping my face, wiping away my tears that don't seem to be stopping any time soon.

"I'm sorry," he murmurs against my lips.

"I got that."

"I love you," he adds quickly, ignoring my sass.

"Took you long enough to say it."

His eyes sear into me and a growl rumbles in his chest. "Where you go, I go."

"You mean that?" I'm almost afraid to ask.

He nods with a slow smile. I seal my lips with his, accepting his apology and everything else he's willing to give me. The bar erupts in hoots and cheers, but I don't care. I love this strong, complicated, brooding man. And he loves me.

I break the kiss and drop my forehead against his and chest, overwhelmed by the joy filling my heart.

I slide my hands to his chest and grab two handfuls of his shirt, my lips twisting up in a teasing simper. "So, guess we should get married then, huh?" I ask, expecting him to laugh. Or run.

Devin's face goes stoic and he pushes me away. My heart skitters to a stop.

"I-I was just kidding," I stammer, kicking myself for ruining the moment with a stupid joke.

"I'm not." A devious grin appears on that beautiful face when Devin drops to one knee in front of me. He fishes a small diamond ring out of his pocket and holds it up. "Told you. I'm all in, hummingbird."

I gasp, at a complete loss for words except for "Holy shit!" My hands are shaking and my tears have started to fall again.

Devin chuckles before swallowing hard. "That a yes?"

I nod, speechless, and he slides the ring onto my trembling finger.

Devin stands, wrapping his arms around my waist and spinning me in the air while I giggle into his neck, inhaling the mouth-watering scent of citrus, gas and man.

He sets me down on weak knees. I shake my head, still in shock. I went from brokenhearted to *engaged* in the length of a single song. It's fast, but it's right. I stare up into those soulful black eyes and smile. "See, I told you, Big Man. This is *so* happening."

Epilogue

Jessie
Seven years later

"Robbie, no!" I shout at my trouble-seeking two-year-old, who's reaching for a screwdriver, eager to poke his own eye out. Dark hair and darker eyes, he's the spitting image of his dad. Good thing too, because he's got so much energy I'd have abandoned him at a Chuck E. Cheese if he weren't so damn cute. Rob, the man he was named after, snatches the tool away in the nick of time, causing a torrential downpour from my little one's eyes.

Hearing my exasperated sigh, Grandpa Rob sweeps up the dramatic toddler. "How about we play with a carburetor? A nice, safe, no-pointy-edges carburetor?" Robbie giggles and grabs for the salt-and-pepper push-broom on Rob's lip. The old man lets out a warm laugh. "I'll take that as a yes."

"Thank you," I mouth, reminding myself to petition for sainthood for him later.

Mandy and Becs sneak into the shop, giggling like schoolgirls.

"Everything all set?" I ask them.

"The sign's up, balloons and everything," Mandy muses.

"Balloons?" I ask with a laugh.

"I know, he's going to hate them!" Becs adds with sinister little-sister amusement.

Mandy tips her head towards the shop. "You going to go get the man of the hour?"

I nod and peer through the window to see Devin and Avery, thick as thieves as usual. Avery looks like me, blonde hair and bright green eyes. But she is most definitely her father's daughter. She's quiet and contemplative, with more patience than I'll ever have. At five, she's more at home under the hood of a car than she is on a playground. I used to dress her in skirts and pretty frilly shirts, but gave up when they all came back torn to shreds or covered in grease. I'd be mad, except it's just too adorable. Mandy made a tiny pair of overalls for Avery and now she wipes her hands on her pants, just like her daddy.

Devin and I had a nice long engagement, waiting over a year until Becs could come back from her Freshman year at Notre Dame to be my maid of honor. We also had a couple busy honeymoon years traveling around while I worked on my grant. But he didn't waste a minute getting me pregnant once we moved back home. Avery was born six months after we moved into our new house. Devin refused to put her down for the first few months and I thought she'd never get the chance to learn to walk. I've never seen him happier than the day he found out he was going to be a dad. Both times, he grinned so wide I thought he was going to hurt himself.

"What'cha workin' on, babe?" I call out to the duo.

"Mommie!" Avery chirps, dashing over to me. I wrap her in a big hug, grease stains be damned.

Devin strolls over, looking as sexy as the first day I saw him – tall, dark and devastatingly handsome. Only this time he's not scowling. He's smiling at me, holding our daughter. He leans down and kisses the tip of my nose.

"You look tired," he scolds.

I let out a sigh at the familiar chiding. "I know. The reopening for the flower shop isn't going according to plan. But once they're up and running, I'll take a week off. I promise."

He groans at my side, accepting my compromise. With Professor P.'s help, I was able to start up a permanent program here at home to help small businesses like our auto shop. It keeps me busy, with every new client bringing a new challenge. Plus, I'm helping people, keeping our community thriving. I love it. But some weeks are longer than others. I still try to do too much at once. I still have trouble saying no. But Devin keeps me balanced, making sure I take time to enjoy our family too.

I hold out my hand to him and try to control the grin. "I've got something to show you."

He growls low and annoyed. My Big Man still hates surprises, but I don't care. He's going to like this one. I drag him out front of the shop, making sure to keep him facing me so he doesn't see the sign until I'm good and ready.

"If the alternator's gone in that piece of junk, I'm getting rid of it. I don't care—"

Mandy, Rob, Becs, my brothers and parents, Sean, Mikey, Shelley and a couple of new guys pop out from behind the cars in the parking lot. We all shout "surprise!" at him in unison.

I spin him around and Devin stares up at the new sign that reads 'Bennett Auto and Repair'. His mouth drops open and his forehead wrinkles in confusion.

"We bought it," I tell him, setting Avery down and letting her run to Auntie Becs, her favorite person in the world after her dad. I do a double take at how close Jamie is standing to Becs and he steps away. I make a mental note to grill them both about that later.

"What?" Devin asks again, dumbfounded.

I wrap my arms around my sexy husband. "We own the shop. Or we will, after a few more years of payments. Rob's retiring, and it's all ours now."

"How? Why?" he asks, a wide smile letting me know it's starting to sink in.

"The how is a very intricate and complicated story that involves me being a little nefarious and keeping secrets from you, so let's not go there. The why is simple. Because it's home."

Devin shakes his head in disbelief. "I love you," he coos.

I giggle. "Yeah, I figured."

A few hours of fun and congratulations later, and our new shop has gone quiet.

"Let's go, kiddos," Mandy's voice calls from the shop door.

Avery cheers from Devin's lap, "We're spending the night with Grandpa and Grandma!"

Devin tucks a strand of her golden hair behind her ear. "Is that so?"

I glance over at Devin. His eyes dance mischievously when I answer, "Yep."

Hugs and goodnight kisses complete, Devin and I are alone. He pushes his sleeves up his arms, leans against the hood of a car and smiles at me. I go weak at the knees at the sexy sight.

"Well, Big Man, what did you have in mind for this evening?" I saunter over to him, stepping between his thick thighs and wrapping my arms around his neck.

He slips his arms around my waist, dipping to my ass as he kisses along my collarbone, sinking lower and lower into my chest. "Well, JB. I was thinking, to christen our new shop, I could fuck you on the hood of this car. For old times' sake. "

"Aren't you sentimental."

He spins us, gripping the outside of my thighs and propping me up on the hood of the car, sliding his hand into my hair and claiming my lips with a devastating kiss. I grab his wrist, holding on for dear life while his kiss consumes me. He tangles his tongue with mine, teasing me with a promise of the pleasure it's going to give me when it heads farther south. Devin moans into my lips, hunger growing within him.

He kisses along my jaw, nipping at my neck with a rough tenderness that makes me love him with every inch of my soul.

"I love the hell out of you, Devin Bennett." I kiss him with everything I have. Everything he's given me. "How about we work on making baby number three?"

"Oh, this is so happening," he groans.

Want to see more like this?
Here's a taster for you to enjoy!

Beautiful Sinners:
Secrets, Lies and Vegas
Pamela L. Todd

Excerpt

Excitement fizzed in my stomach as I followed the girls, who talked a million miles a minute and barely paused to take a breath. We walked into the restaurant...or was it a circus tent? Soft, floaty material of all colors was our ceiling and the wall panels displayed vintage art from the big tops of days gone by. In fact, the only clue that we hadn't stepped into a 1940s circus was the window that overlooked the world-famous fountain display. It took my breath away even in daylight, but now, lit up against the backdrop of darkness, I could barely tear my eyes away.

Hayley introduced us to the hostess, who led us to our table, the most central in the restaurant. Eve scanned the room, her hunter instincts on full alert as she surveyed her prey. Beth looped arms with hers, giggling in her ear.

The moment our waiter appeared, Hayley ordered a bottle of champagne.

"Well, I think we should make a toast," Hayley announced once our glasses had been filled.

"Here, here," Eve said, raising her glass. "To Marley! For without her, I would never have met that cute investment banker from Chicago."

Hayley rolled her eyes. "Yes, Eve, that was exactly what I was thinking."

Beth giggled, flipping her long, shiny black hair over one shoulder. "Yeah, because it should be about Ken from Kentucky."

I snorted a laugh. "You do remember that his name wasn't actually Ken? And the fact that he only put up with the nickname was because you left your bra pinned to the wall in Coyote Ugly and he could see your nipples through your dress?"

Beth waggled her eyebrows. "Well, I do have very nice nipples."

"You should send that to Hallmark," Hayley said. "Okay, in all seriousness guys, I really do want to make a toast to Marley."

Beth and Eve raised their glasses, eyes on Hayley as they waited for her toast.

"Marley, you know we love you," Hayley said with a smile, "and I think it goes without saying that this trip has been ridiculously overdue. So here's to our last night, and going as hard as we can."

"To Marley!" Beth and Eve chorused, chinking their glasses at mine.

I forced a smile and took a gulp of champagne, which tasted sour on my tongue. That toast, whilst heartfelt, felt like a needle in my heart. It was just another reminder of how different I was from my friends.

Eve tossed back the remainder of her drink. As she placed the empty glass on the table, her eyes darted between us all when she noticed us staring. "What are you all looking at? You said go hard."

"I said hard, not sloppy," Hayley said, shaking her head, the small smile pulling at her lips, ruining any scolding she may have intended. She tugged on the end of Eve's shoulder-length blonde hair. "You might want to pin this up before bed, because no one will be holding it back for you."

Eve leaned closer to Hayley, pursing her glossy red lips. "Honey, I plan on burning all the alcohol out of my system with vigorous exercise."

Beth laughed. "Let's make a toast to that!"

We ordered our food when the waiter returned, Beth and Eve still sizing up their potential prey. I circled the rim of my glass with my fingertip and felt a set of eyes on me. Hayley studied me with her curious blue eyes, a tiny crease between her eyebrows.

Out of everyone, it was Hayley I was closest to, the first out of this group of girls I'd met. They pulled me into their orbit in a blur of cocktails and club music. Beneath the man-eating exterior of these women were big hearts and kinder spirits. I adored them all, but Hayley was the one I felt the deepest bond with. But like any close relationship, it had its perks and its downsides. Like right now, when I knew she could see more than the others.

"Last night blues?" she asked, her tone light.

I gave a swift nod. "Something like that."

Hayley patted my knee under the table. "We'd better make it a memorable one then, hadn't we?"

"It's already been pretty memorable, Hayley," I said, giving her a genuine smile.

And it had.

Surprisingly.

None of us had been to Vegas before and I had been hesitant to come. *Sin City...* Who wanted to go there? A city where people flocked to make stupid decisions and change their lives…for better or worse.

Maybe that isn't such a bad idea…

I wasn't altogether sure what I'd expected of this place. When the plane had begun its descent toward the ground and I'd seen the bright lights of this unusual world, a flicker of excitement had rumbled low in my body. I'd all seen the movies, the TV shows, but really, nothing could have prepared me for the intensity of Vegas. I'd had my preconceived ideas, the mental image that was a far cry from the glossy, fluorescent reality. I'd thought I'd known what to expect, but it wasn't until we'd driven down the Strip with the lights reflecting off the windows that I'd discovered there wasn't actually anything — real or imagined — that could have prepared me for Vegas herself.

It felt like I was a Lilliputian in a glittery and exotic setting — only the buildings were Gulliver, and these were *my* travels. Truth was, I had looked down my nose at the thought of a trip to Las Vegas. I wasn't a snob. It was just the white-trash stories that went hand in hand with the city which made it a less than desirable vacation spot. But when I'd got here, I couldn't have been more wrong.

Wealth and luxury screamed from most places and it was larger than life. A playground for those looking for an escape from reality, even for a short while.

Maybe this was exactly where I needed to be.

After a delicious meal that was served on a plate with pictures of monkeys, the girls tried to decide where to go for the night's activities. Well, Hayley tried to narrow down the options — Eve and Beth were still admiring the specimens on display. I, on the other hand, ogled the dessert tray.

God, I hate diets.

Beth subtly pointed out a target to Eve. "Look at that one, over there."

"Oooh...." Eve crooned.

"Oh! That one!"

"Oh my God, are you serious? What are you, blind?"

"Over there then."

"Mmm-hmm."

"Wait a minute... I've got it... By the bar. See?"

"Dibs."

"You can't call dibs!"

"I just did!"

"But I saw him first!"

"Then you should have called it."

"Fine. Whatever. I don't care."

"You so do."

Beth and Eve's shameful game of man window shopping was a welcome distraction. It was an impressive feat that they found so many desirable men in the restaurant, considering there were only nineteen tables. When I'd first met them, I'd thought the guys they favored were lucky to have such beautiful girls fawning over them. Now I felt sorry for the poor bastards. It was like watching a lioness flirt with an innocent springbok. There was no doubt that these girls were predators—and they were hungry.

They thought of this vacation as a buffet table, and the helpless male habitants and visitors of Vegas were the only meat on the menu. I'd lost count of how many business cards and cocktail napkins with carefully written phone numbers they'd acquired this weekend. With tonight being our last night, they would be bringing their A game...and no one was safe.

Hayley giggled, breaking my reverie, and leaned over the table to whisper, "A guy at the bar is staring at you."

My eyebrows shot up "So?"

She rolled her eyes. "So go talk to him!"

"Yeah. Right," I said, folding my arms across my chest.

Hayley frowned. "Why not?"

"I can think of a few reasons." Maybe it was because Hayley had made me aware, but I felt a pair of eyes on me. The little hairs on the back of neck stood on end and it was all I could do not to turn around.

Hayley gave a slight shake of her head, as though admitting I was a lost cause. "So where are we going?" she asked, the question aimed for no one specific.

"I really want to go back to Coyote Ugly," Beth pleaded, clasping her hands together under her chin and pouting.

Eve arched a perfect eyebrow at our friend. "And lose another bra to the wall? Good thing we're only here for the weekend. Imagine the loss if we were here for longer."

I rolled my eyes. "Please. Like Beth needs an excuse to buy new underwear."

"We are so not going back to Coyote Ugly. Come on, you guys. We need to make this a stellar night." Hayley's eyes flickered to me. "For Marley's sake."

I frowned. "Why for Marley's sake?"

Beth shot me a pointed look. "Like we could get you on another vacation. It was hard enough getting you to come this time!"

I dropped my eyes, unable to look at their accusing faces. Though they were messing around, I doubted they would ever know how much their words stung. How quickly they forgot the easiness of their own lives.

Hayley cleared her throat. "Guys, focus. Where are we headed next? We've already been sitting in here for more than two hours. And I nominate Marley to be in charge of tonight's festivities."

"Why don't we just stay in the hotel tonight?" I suggested. We were staying in one of the best hotels on the Strip, yet we hadn't even experienced its nightclub yet.

Hayley nodded her agreement. "Vault? Yeah, I heard it's meant to be one of the best. We're staying here anyway. May as well keep close to home."

Beth looked disappointed at being outvoted, but when a group of well-dressed and devastatingly good-looking men walked past our table voicing their own plans to visit the same club, she soon perked up.

Beth wriggled in her chair. "You guys done?"

Home of Erotic Romance

Sign up for our newsletter and find out about all our romance book releases, eBook sales and promotions, sneak peeks and FREE romance books!

About the Author

Amelia Kingston is many things, the most interesting of which are probably California girl, writer, traveler, and dog mom. She survives on chocolate, coffee, wine, and sarcasm. Not necessarily in that order.

She's been blessed with a patient husband who's embraced her nomad ways and traveled with her to over 30 countries across 5 continents (I'm coming for you next, Antarctica!). She's also been cursed with an impatient (although admittedly adorable) terrier who pouts when her dinner is 5 minutes late.

She writes about strong, stubborn, flawed women and the men who can't help but love them. Her irreverent books aim to be silly and fun with the occasional storm cloud to remind us to appreciate the sunny days. As a hopeless romantic, her favorite stories are the ones that remind us all that while love is rarely perfect, it's always worth chasing.

Amelia loves to hear from readers. You can find her contact information, website details and author profile page at https://www.totallybound.com